The Cowboy's Hunt

The Cowboy's Hunt

A Three Sisters Ranch Romance

Jamie K. Schmidt

The Cowboy's Hunt

Tule Publishing First Printing, July 2019

The Tule Publishing, Inc.

First Publication by Tule Publishing 2019

Cover design by Llewellen Designs

ISBN: 978-1-951190-13-2

Prologue

July 2019

EMILY SULLIVAN WAS glad to be back in the States. She wasn't sure how she felt about being back at the Three Sisters Ranch, though. Tired, she decided. She felt tired. And hungry. Worst of all, she could smell the bacon her mother was making in the kitchen. Her stomach roiled and she forced herself to breathe through her mouth.

But the reek of it was worth it to see her sisters and parents leap up from the table and surround her.

"Why didn't you let us pick you up from the airport?" her oldest sister, Kelly, asked. She looked as beautiful as ever, like the rodeo queen she had been.

"I'm so glad you're here. Now we can get started." Janice, her other older sister, hugged her and then went back to her notebook, where she probably had a seven-page to-do list. Janice looked like a badass librarian who could wield a ruler like a samurai sword if you pissed her off.

"You're too skinny," her mother lamented. She and Alissa, Kelly's daughter, were dusted with flour from baking something that smelled much nicer than the animal meat. After a rough start, her mother had fallen into grandmother mode like it was her job.

"It's good to see you, baby girl." Her father hugged her hard.

When did he get so frail? He had aged ten years since she last saw him at Christmas.

"You've got nothing to worry about," she told him fiercely, gripping him tight.

A few weeks ago, she had been working in West Tigray, Ethiopia, when the sporadic internet service in the town she was staying in delivered a cryptic message from her father.

Come home one last time. We're selling the ranch. We can't keep up with the bills.

She had joined the Peace Corps out of college because she wanted to make a difference and she hadn't come home because she hadn't felt like she had managed that yet. But she always thought there would be a home to come home to. She had always dreamed of taking over as ranch manager from her father when he retired. But her family had never taken her seriously. She was the baby, the wild child, the practical joker. Emily had thought that serving a few years in the Peace Corps would lend some weight to how serious she was about running the Three Sisters Ranch.

"How can you run a cattle ranch when you're a vegetarian?" her father would scoff every time she had tried to bring up the subject after she graduated high school.

Selling cattle to the slaughterhouse wasn't her favorite part of ranch life, that was for sure. But when she was in charge, she could diversify the ranch so they didn't have to rely on that so much. And she could make sure the animals were treated humanely until it was time to sell them. What happened after that wasn't something she liked to think about, but she would have to face the reality of it sooner or later. Or maybe she would change them from a cattle ranch to a dairy ranch, but that was an argument for another day.

The Three Sisters was a five-thousand-acre cattle ranch in Last Stand, Texas. It had been in their family for generations. But once Emily had been born, her father changed the name from the Sullivan Ranch to the Three Sisters in honor of his daughters.

"I've got my girls home," he said, opening up his embrace to include her niece, Alissa.

Her family could be overwhelming and after the isolation and vastness of Africa, Emily was feeling a little claustrophobic with all the activity that was going on in the kitchen. She was having a hard time wrapping her head around that it was morning. In Ethiopia, it would be around four in the afternoon.

"So, what did I miss?" Emily held her father out at arm's length to look at him again. He didn't look well. Did her sisters keep anything from her? They had arrived a few weeks ago, while she dealt with the red tape to get back home. She had been eight months into her second contracted term with the Peace Corps and had to apply for a hardship dismissal so she didn't lose the stipend she had earned. One of the terms of the negotiation was that she had to stay and train her replacement. And while Kelly and Janice texted her as often as they could, Emily wasn't sure she'd got all the messages.

"We're reorganizing a bit," her father said gruffly.

"The cattle industry is dying. We need to branch out into more sustainable activities," Emily said.

He chucked her under the chin. "You're so cute."

Emily grimaced. "I've killed men for less."

He snorted. "See what I mean?"

"That *is* kind of condescending, Dad," Janice said.

"You're cute, too," he told her.

"I'm cute," Janice said to Kelly, who rolled her eyes.

"So am I!" Alissa piped up, and they all chuckled. Her niece was five years old and had just attended her first rodeo. Emily had missed the annual Last Stand Rodeo that happened over Fourth of July week, but she got to see the video of Alissa mutton bustin'. Kelly had taken a ton of pictures to build up her portfolio for the portrait studio she was planning on opening. After looking at her album, it was almost like Emily had been there.

"Wait until you meet Trent and Donovan," her mother said. "They're such nice men."

"So I've heard," Emily said with a trace of sarcasm. Both nice men were renting land from her father and it was helping keep the creditors at bay, but it wasn't a long-term solution.

Trent Campbell was a local boy who had made it big in professional bull riding. He was back in town and starting his own rodeo school on their land. It was supposed to have been a surprise that her father had wanted to spring on them, but her sisters had ferreted out the truth and filled her in.

Emily thought that was pretty cool. She remembered seeing Trent ride when they'd gone to the rodeos when she was growing up. However, she knew it bothered her father to have strangers on his land.

The other renter, however, she had major problems with—even though she'd never met him. Donovan Link had paid for hunting rights on their land and was currently paying a monthly lease on the property until he decided if he wanted to build a hunting lodge. That was going to happen over her dead body. She had to convince Donovan that it wasn't worth his time to be here. Her family would figure out how to make up the lost revenue another way.

"I saw Trent's school as I drove by. I'm hoping we won't have to deal with another building and more foot traffic." Emily figured she'd try to get on her father's good side.

"Well, hope again," Janice snapped. "My retreat center is going to bring in groups of people and since Kelly's photo studio will be a part of it, we all have to realize that changes are going to happen. And we all need to adjust to them."

Great, not home five minutes and she'd already touched a nerve. "I didn't mean your retreat center," Emily said. "I meant nonfamily members."

Kelly smiled into her coffee. "You mean Donovan's proposed hunting lodge."

Her sisters were her best friends—when they weren't trying to be a second and third mom to her. Talk about bossy! Kelly had always been on her to fix her hair and makeup, while Janice wanted to quiz her on history and math flash cards. And yet, they covered for her when she had missed curfew and looked the other way when she signed her father up to get *Ms. Magazine.*

They hadn't had a lot of adult time together, though. Kelly had decided to move to New York after a fight with their dad and Janice went to Kentucky straight out of college.

Emily had planned on sticking around and going to a local college for a business degree, but her father had refused to take her seriously. So, she had decided to go on an adventure instead. Africa had been the farthest point she could get to. And since no one knew her there, Emily had finally been free of her family's expectations.

In Africa, she had been a "case manager," instead of "the baby." She was an American worker, not Kelly Sullivan's little sister. Emily had taken care of children and planted food. She had not sent cattle out to be slaughtered in the name of profit, and she certainly didn't hunt for fun.

"We don't need a hunting lodge here. It's barbaric."

Frank Sullivan rolled his eyes. "He's going to help us out with our feral hog problem."

Emily grit her teeth and with effort kept the smile on her face. "We can trap them. We don't have to kill them."

"Just because you don't want to eat pork, don't take that away from the rest of us," he said.

"Dad," she complained. It wasn't about that and he knew it. Ever since she was little, she couldn't stand the thought of an animal being in pain or being killed. It made growing up on a cattle ranch tough. Emily had to accept that there were situations that weren't ideal, but necessary, until she took over the ranch from her father. In her opinion, though, a hunting lodge wasn't one of them.

"Look, let's say you do trap them," her father said. "What are you going to do with them? Relocate them? Where? No one is going to want them. Give them to someone else to slaughter and eat? It's the same thing."

She didn't have a leg to stand on with the feral hogs and she knew it. She didn't have to like it, though. But she also knew that most hunters weren't just interested in pigs. "I agree the feral hogs are a problem. Are the other game animals off-limits?" Emily challenged.

"Deer are also a nuisance. Turkey, too."

"Why can't we coexist with nature and show tourists the spectacular wildlife we have? Wildlife that's still alive." Emily knew she was talking just to hear her own voice. Her family was exchanging "there she goes again" looks. She had been hoping her sisters would be on her side in this matter. But she probably lost them when she mouthed off about the new buildings. Her family took for granted all the species of animals that shared their ranch with them, from the cute little javelinas to the majestic elks. There was so much to enjoy about them. It didn't have to be survival of the fittest. They could all coexist—if her family could find a way to stop foreclosure. The fact that selling cattle to the slaughterhouse was no longer paying all their bills was a big red flag that things needed to change. And she was just the ranch manager to do that.

Through her spotty internet and trying to find her way home from Africa, Emily and her sisters had brainstormed several ways to bring the ranch back into the black. Kelly was eventually planning on opening up a portrait studio, but for right now, she was doing staged shots of kids on horseback and engagement photos against the gorgeous Texas sunsets. Janice was setting up an area for a women's retreat, a kind of a dudette ranch, which was going to drive Nate, the ranch's foreman, crazy. But since Nate had always had a soft spot for Janice, her sister was hoping she could get him on board with the plan.

Emily had a bunch of ideas. One of them was to have a wildlife conservation museum, although she didn't think it was going to be a moneymaker for the ranch. It would be nice to have a place to celebrate nature. And it would be one more thing for Janice's guests to do. However, she had a number to call that her friend Bobby in the Peace Corps gave her to contact someone about using their land for alternative energy sources. The ranch had a few unused pastures that could support several wind turbines to harness wind power. And after a small initial investment, brokering the energy could sustain the farm in perpetuity. Emily knew her father was going to be a hard sell on it, but she thought it would work. Saving the farm by using renewable energy would give her a small victory over her family who thought she was nutty when she preached conservation.

"Your mother told me what you girls have planned, and I'm all for it," her father said. "The problem is each of your bright ideas is going to cost money that we don't have. To be honest, you all should have done this a few years ago."

Typical Daddy. Of course, he didn't tell any of them about the ranch being in trouble until last month. "Well, we didn't," Emily said. "But we're here now."

"Donovan and Trent brought their own money in, so they get first dibs on the land and resources." Frank sat back down at the table to finish his breakfast. "I want you girls to work with them, not against them."

Emily glanced away and hoped he didn't see that she had her fingers crossed. While she wasn't thrilled about bull riding, she could live with it as long as the bulls weren't being abused. The hunting, though? Donovan Link had to go.

"Can I get you some blueberry pancakes?" her mom asked.

"I'd love some," she said gratefully. "Butter and syrup will make everything better."

"I thought you couldn't eat butter because it comes from a cow," her father challenged her.

Emily sighed at this old argument. "I'm a vegetarian, Dad. Not a vegan. Although, if Mom has some vegan butter, I'd be glad to have that instead."

"Wouldn't matter," Kelly said around a mouthful of pancake. "She put butter, eggs, and milk in the recipe."

And that was another reason why she wasn't vegan. It was damn near impossible to be one in this family.

Chapter One

September 2019

SALT LICKS WERE fascist. Emily glared up at the tree stand and then back down to the stump where the large block of solid salt was perched. That wasn't hunting. That was waiting. You sat up all comfortable in your perch and waited for an unsuspecting deer to wander over and take a lick of the tasty treat. Then blamo! Bambi's an orphan.

Looking around, Emily didn't see any deer or hunters for that matter. Picking up the bait, she put it into the large rucksack bag she had on her back. Emily couldn't stop Donovan Link from hunting on her family's land, but she could even up the odds a bit.

Realistically, she knew she couldn't cover the one hundred and twenty-five acres her father had leased to him that bordered state forest land, but it wasn't in her nature to just sit back and let hunters kill animals. Getting back on her horse, Sunflower, she continued through the dust and the scrub brush looking for more bait traps.

Her persistence paid off, and after about a half hour in the saddle and squinting up into the trees, she found another tree stand. Sliding off the back of Sunflower, she patted her horse's neck and watched as she ambled over to the pond to take a drink of water. The grass had patches of green with brown around the tree. It had been a blistering summer and some of the grass hadn't survived. She didn't see any salt licks. Taking a long glug from her canteen, Emily figured it had to be around here somewhere. Why else sit up in a tree stand if you didn't expect something to come wandering by? As soon as she found it, though, she had to hurry back home. Her mother was making a vegetable lasagna especially for her, and there would be hell to pay if she was late.

Glancing back at Sunflower, she figured the mare would stay put for a bit. Emily should have taken the Gator, their secondhand all-terrain vehicle, or borrowed Nate's truck, but she didn't want there to be evidence of her thievery.

After walking around the area and still coming up empty, Emily went deeper into the woods. Her eyes on the ground, she pushed away scrub brushes and stepped over ruts. Her father wasn't kidding about the feral pigs being a problem. They had done a number on the trees and the ground. If they got into the cattle pastures, their cows would have a hard time finding food. The ranch would have to buy more hay and grains to supplement—and that would cut into the ranch's dwindling bottom line.

As Emily continued to look around, she heard some rustling and crashing from the underbrush ahead. Squinting into the distance, she didn't see anything, but she made her way back toward the tree. The noise got louder and she peered over her shoulder. Thundering toward her was a large hog, grunting and snorting. Enormous and ugly, it bore down on her, moving swiftly for its size.

Shit.

Emily turned on her heel and sprinted for the tree. Planks had been nailed to the tree to form a ladder up to the tree stand. She was a few steps up it before the hog caught up to her. Lunging at the tree, it leapt for her. Its tusks grazed her ankles and the material on her boots tore. Emily swung to the left, almost losing her grip. She knew that more than a nasty fall would await her if she let go. The animal's grunts and squeals helped her get her footing out of sheer panic, and she scrambled up onto the platform. Lying prone, she stared down at the beast. Emily grimaced as it rocked its body against the trunk, as if it wanted to push the tree down.

"Go away," she yelled. She was much braver thirty feet above it. A whirring and clicking sound caught her attention and she found herself staring into a game camera that had been pointed at the ground. "Please tell me that wasn't just recorded for posterity?" Or worse. Her family. Her father had just gotten out of the hospital and rehab from his second heart attack. With his temper, he would blow a gasket if he saw what she had been up to.

And if this was Donovan's camera—which it surely was—it probably wasn't the only one and that meant she was more than likely busted for stealing his salt licks. The good news was, he was probably on his way to rescue her from the boar right now. The bad news was, he was going to be insufferable.

They had spent the last few months as adversaries, with her going from being outright hostile to him, to trying to kill him with kindness. Nothing worked. He had skin thicker than the hog below her. Then, they had come to an understanding of sorts, a wary détente. Donovan could be a charmer when he wanted to be, and Emily found it hard to breathe when he smiled at her instead of scowled.

He wasn't immune to her either. Emily had caught him looking at her when he thought she wasn't aware of it. Just for shits and giggles, she had convinced him to go zip-lining with her. She was surprised that he was just as big of an adrenaline junkie as she was. They had such a good time one-upping each other, they had made it a weekly occurrence to do something that would have turned her mother's hair white if she had known about it.

Bungee jumping. Off-roading. And skydiving. Next week, they were going to go on a hot air balloon ride.

They weren't really dates. But if he hadn't been a hunter, they could have been. She had a good time with him, despite what he did for a living. Lately, though, Emily had stopped thinking of him as an adversary. She'd started to notice little things, like how he had laugh lines at the corners of his eyes and his cheeks got five-o'clock shadow on them by midafternoon.

Donovan Link was beginning to be a distraction and she didn't like that it distracted her from her mission to stop him from hunting on her family's land.

Now that his hunting lodge had been built, the best Emily could do was inconvenience him and delay the inevitable. And try not to think about how nice his butt looked in faded Wranglers.

Below her, the hog rubbed his full length against the tree, knocking off one of the boards that served as part of the ladder up the tree.

"Shoo," she said, considering dumping the salt lick from her bag on top of the hog. Its rough shoulder skin was like armor and it would bounce right off it, but it might give the big bastard the idea to leave. Instead of heeding her instructions, however, he burrowed his snout deeper into the dirt. As she watched, four more pigs of varying sizes came out and started rooting around the tree.

Groaning, she pulled herself into a sitting position and glanced around the tree stand. This one had a camp chair and a large cooler filled with everything from a first aid kit to extra bottles of water and granola bars. She sat in the camp chair and took out her phone. Emily wasn't surprised that she didn't have a signal. Who was she going to call anyway? She didn't want her family to come all the way out here. She wasn't risking the lecture for a rescue—she'd rather stay in a tree all night.

After a particularly loud shouting match with Donovan a few weeks ago, her mother pulled her aside and told her in no uncertain terms that she was embarrassing the family and that it was time to grow up. It stung, probably because her mother had been right. Then Sarah Sullivan reminded her that this was her father's land and her father's decision and she didn't want to get on the wrong side of him. Since he once kicked her sister Kelly out when she was six months pregnant, Emily knew what he was capable of. Although a part of her was sure he'd never do that to her. To him, she was still the baby of the family—even though Alissa now had that honor.

Trent, who was now her sister Kelly's fiancé, was still recovering from having his leg shattered after he was thrown by a bull. He could bring the truck to rescue her. He might be convinced to keep her secret. But there was no way he would keep a secret from Kelly. And then the lecture would come from Kelly, who forgot that Emily was her sister and not her daughter when it came to scolding. Besides, Kelly was no angel no matter how much domestic bliss Trent was showering down on her.

Their ranch foreman, Nate, would come and get her if she called him. But then, everyone would know she had been screwing around on the land her dad had leased Donovan. The ranch hands loved Donovan. He was their poker buddy and the guy who supplied them with pork for their weekly barbecues. Emily couldn't risk being hated by them. She'd never be able to get anything done around the ranch. Eventually, when she took over for her father and ran the ranch, she would need their support.

Of course, every time she mentioned it to her father, he dismissed it and said something sexist like she'd be better off looking to be a rancher's wife. Or that women couldn't keep up with men on a cattle drive, which didn't make any sense. He was the one who demanded she and her sisters could pull their weight alongside the ranch hands.

Emily knew she had a long way to go before she could even think about stepping up and taking on more responsibility around here. She wanted to be business savvy and a professional rancher. She didn't want to be a rancher's wife. She wanted to run the whole damn thing.

Her father thought that was cute.

She was going to have to hope that when Donovan came to gloat, he wouldn't tell her father about her antics. Because nothing destroys your credibility to be a professional businesswoman than petty thievery and sabotage.

Perhaps she should have thought this through before she acted out.

"Can you hurry up?" she said to the camera. Maybe if she annoyed him, he'd come faster so he could bawl her out. "I'm sorry," she whispered. Emily knew there was no way she was going to live this down. What was worse, she was going to have to witness Donovan shooting the hogs.

Emily didn't want to think about that. She took a hopeful look downward. Maybe the boars had gone away. But no such luck. In fact, more were coming and heading toward the pond, tearing up the ground as they went. She knew they were destructive and dangerous, but she didn't want to see them killed.

She hoped that Sunflower would have the good sense to stay away. The horse knew her way back to the ranch, but Emily still fretted about her. The hogs probably wouldn't attack the horse, but nothing was certain.

When Sunflower screamed, Emily nearly fell out of the tree. Listening desperately, she heard retreating hoofbeats and could only hope that Sunflower would outrun the hogs. She heard squeals and wondered if the hogs were chasing her beautiful horse.

Sharp rifle shots broke the relative silence of the late afternoon, and Emily covered her ears. She counted five quick shots. Then five more. Her breathing came in short, panicked pants and she blinked to keep the tears back. The hogs at the foot of the tree scattered, but she was shaking too hard to climb down. Had Sunflower survived?

Emily knew the rifle shots had to be from Donovan. What was taking him so long? Was Sunflower all right? Emily started to climb down, but wondered if she should just stay put. She didn't want to miss Donovan and have to walk all the way back to the ranch at sunset, even though it probably would serve her right. It would be dark by the time she got back. Settling back on the camp chair, she snitched a granola bar and ate it, wishing it was her mother's zucchini lasagna instead.

Much later, she heard an engine approaching and sure enough, Donovan Link walked into her line of sight.

"You can come down now," he drawled. "The coast is clear."

Donovan Link looked like a Hemsworth brother working as an L.L.Bean model, posing for the camera. When he flashed a grin, it made her choke on air. He looked like a movie version of a big game hunter and Emily should hate him on principle. But he wasn't a stereotypical trophy-mad jerk with a gun. And God, did that piss her off. In his own way, he was just as concerned about conservation as she was. But nothing she'd said or done these past few months could convince him to stop his hunts. He'd built his hunting lodge and had signed a three-year contract with her father.

"Where's my horse?" she asked, aware that her voice was trembling. If something happened to Sunflower, she'd never forgive herself.

"Heading hell-bent for leather back to the barn last time I saw her."

"Do you think she made it?" Emily took a shaky breath.

"I think she might have got cut up some by the brush and brambles, but yeah I think she's all right. Do you want me to come up there and get you?"

"No," she said sharply. "I can do it." That was the last thing she needed—to be rescued like a fairy princess from his tree stand.

With her fingers shaking, Emily forced herself to climb down. When her boots were firmly on the ground, she had to rein in the urge to throw herself into Donovan's arms.

"Are you all right?" he asked, frowning at her ruined boot.

"Yeah," she said and forced herself to meet his eyes. "Can we get out of here?"

He gestured for her to go in front of him and she noticed that he carried his rifle as easily as if it were a part of his arm.

"Did you kill the hogs?"

"Why are you asking questions that will upset you?" he said. "Just don't look in the back of the truck."

Emily stopped dead in her tracks. "The hogs are in the back of your truck?" For a moment, she wondered how he got them to run up into the back of the pickup, and then she realized she was an idiot. Forcing herself to get into the cab of the truck, she shuddered at the senseless loss of life.

Donovan secured the rifle in the gun rack behind them, reversed the truck, and headed back toward the ranch.

Emily couldn't stand the silence any longer. "Thank you," she said.

"You're welcome."

She waited for him to launch into an "I told you so" speech about the dangers of the hog population or to justify his killing of them. But he didn't.

"What are you going to do with the…?" Emily couldn't finish her sentence.

"They're dressed, so I was going to run them down to The Hut." He looked over at her. "I don't suppose you want to join me?"

Pressing her lips tightly together, she shook her head.

"Shame. I think you at least owe me a beer."

She owed him more than that. "Are you going to tell my father about this?"

"I don't think I need to, do you?"

"No."

More dreadful silence.

"Are you going to tell my sisters?"

"Not my place. But Janice will probably wonder how Sunflower got hurt. And Nate's going to wonder why I took off in a hurry."

"How many cameras do you have out there?" she asked, trying for nonchalance.

"Enough," he said.

Emily closed her eyes. Busted. "Salt licks are cheating." She sounded defensive instead of righteous. Damn it.

"When you're paying $300 a day to bag a deer, you get mighty testy if you don't see one. And mighty testy hunters don't come back, and they certainly don't tell their friends about what a wonderful time they had."

"It's barbaric," she whispered, but without heat.

"Circle of life, sweetheart."

Glaring at him, she crossed her arms. "Tell that to Bambi."

He snorted. "We're after the bucks. Not the mommy deer."

"Did you just say 'mommy deer'?"

Donovan continued on as if she hadn't interrupted him. "And they're eating up your cattle's food and your mother's garden. But you know all of that already, so why are you busting my balls about it?"

"I don't agree with what you do."

"You don't have to. But you do have to stop stealing my property and you do have to stay off my land."

"It's not your land."

"It is, as long as your father has leased it to me for hunting. He wants me to thin the population because there's not enough food to sustain all the deer and hogs. Not to mention the destruction they're causing."

"Can't you trap them? Relocate them?"

"The trapped animals go to the slaughterhouse. You can't relocate them because they're an invasive species. All of which, again, you already know. It prolongs their terror and it isn't a humane or clean kill."

She winced. "I don't want to talk about it."

"You don't have to. You just have to stay out of my way."

"Fine," Emily said. And this time relished the silence until they made it onto the paved driveway that Janice had installed for her retreat clients. Then dread filled her. She had missed dinner. Her horse was still missing and she was going to have to talk fast to keep her father from losing his cool. The doctors said he had to take it easy and keep calm. And with his infamous temper, that was not going to be easy.

Donovan drove her up to the ranch house. "Leave the salt lick," he said, placing the truck into park.

Digging into her bag, she dropped it on the seat.

"I hope you saw how dangerous it can be going out around sunset without a rifle."

She sighed. Here was the lecture. "I got the message. I learned my lesson."

"That'll be the day," he muttered.

She narrowed her eyes at him, but forced herself to remember that he wasn't ratting her out or pressing charges or anything else that he had a right to do because she had acted like a brat. "I'm sorry," she said again. "I truly know better, but I seem to lose all sense when I'm around you."

"Pardon me?" He turned to face her, raising an eyebrow.

She slugged him in the arm. "Cut it out. I'm trying to do the right thing here. I'm sorry. It won't happen again. Thank you for being decent about it and for not telling my family what a dumbass I was." Then before she could think better of it, she leaned in and kissed him quick on the cheek.

It should have been the cheek, but the son of a bitch

turned his head at the last minute and she got him on the lips. It was like static electricity jolted through her and the kiss was less of a peck and more of a sultry smooch. She pulled back, feeling the heat rising to her cheeks. Fumbling with the door handle, she nearly pitched out of the truck on her ass.

"Anytime," he drawled.

She managed not to slam the door.

Chapter Two

DONOVAN LINK LOOKED around the hunting lodge he had built on Frank Sullivan's land. He hadn't wanted to put more money in a place that he wasn't sure he was going to stay for very long, but if he wanted to bring in the big spenders, he needed to give them a place to drink and sleep. It was rustic, though. Pine wood and leather, built for practicality not luxury. Just like him.

But his clientele wasn't paying him to stay at the Ritz. They were paying him to lead them to where the action was. Although he had to admit, it was nice to stay in a room that he had designed and built. It beat the hell out of the endless stream of motels he grew up in. He designed the hunting lodge so his office was on the ground floor, but his bedroom was through a door behind it. It appealed to his workaholic side.

He'd almost consider putting roots down at the Three Sisters Ranch if it weren't for two things. One: the ranch was teetering on bankruptcy. And two: Emily Sullivan.

Emily Sullivan was a bitty thing to be such an eco-warrior, but she could give Rambo a run for his money in fierceness. Her face lit up with the passion of a devoted zealot when she talked about saving the planet, saving the endangered species, and of course, saving her family's ranch. But in the quiet moments, he could see that her heart was pure and she truly believed that this world was worth saving. Life had taught him it was only a matter of time before reality crushed her. For some insane reason, he didn't want to be around when that happened.

She was determined to run him off her father's land. Normally, he'd cut his losses and go. But she brought out the ornery in him and he doubled down and decided to give her a run for *her* money. Not to mention, she looked sexy as hell when she was all fired up. He'd come close to kissing her several times on their weekly adventures, but he was afraid it would ruin things. Still, he had some powerful fantasies going on about her and in most of them, she wasn't thinking about hunting at all.

"Have you seen her yet?" Nate Pierson asked him, coming inside the hunting lodge with his Australian shepherd, Daisy, after a hard day of cattle ranching. Nate was the foreman of the Three Sisters Ranch and came over every Friday for beer and poker nights with some of the ranch hands if Donovan didn't have an early morning hunt planned the next day.

For a moment, he thought Nate was talking about Emily and he almost replied that he hadn't seen the pain in his ass today. But then he realized Nate was talking about the white elk. He was almost positive that Nate and the boys were pulling his chain about that. In all of his years in Texas, he had never seen a white elk.

"Not yet," Donovan drawled, trying to spot in Nate's expression if he was bullshitting him or not. But from what he could tell, Nate either believed in the white elk or he bluffed better when he wasn't playing poker. "I heard a couple of bucks bugling down by the pond, but the damned hogs are driving them away. I'm going to have to use the truck and ATVs instead of horses this week. I don't want to risk them bolting or getting hurt." Donovan pet Daisy as she trotted past him to the water bowl he placed out for her and Emily's sister Janice's six dogs.

"Watch out for the mud."

Donovan stifled a groan. That was all he needed—to get stuck in the mud with a team of overzealous hunters.

"How many do you have coming?" Nate asked.

"Six."

Nate whistled. "Good haul. If you keep that up for the rest of the year, you'll have this paid off in no time." He patted the wall.

"That's the plan," Donovan said. "As long as Emily stops with the nonsense."

"That one's always been wild."

"I don't mind wild. I mind her protesting my business." Last hunt she stood outside the hunting lodge as they were heading out with a sign that said "Meat is Murder." The hunters in his party laughed at her. What was she expecting? These guys paid twenty-five hundred dollars to spend the weekend so they could stock their freezers with venison and pork. At least she'd stopped trying to sabotage his hunting blinds and tree stands. After her stunt a few weeks ago, Emily had been unusually inactive. It felt like the calm before the storm. He almost missed their battle of wills. But luckily, he'd got his Emily fix in when they went hot air ballooning on Monday morning.

It could have been romantic if he hadn't half expected her to try to push him out of the gondola. But when the pilot fired the propane burners, the unexpected noise had caused Emily to jump into his arms. He'd held her for a good minute before they'd both come to their senses. She had felt nice in his arms. He wouldn't mind holding her again.

"She'll find something else to occupy herself once she realizes she's wasting her time."

"I hope so."

"She's going to the bank tomorrow to see if she can get a loan to buy her wind turbines. That should keep her out of your hair."

Donovan wasn't sure any bank in their right mind would give an unemployed twenty-three-year-old that kind of money, but he saw how determined Emily was when she put her mind to something. If anyone could convince a stodgy old banker to trust her, it would be her.

"I'm going to go the H-E-B to pick up some beer for the weekend. You want to take a ride?"

"Nah, I'm beat. I'm going to grab a hot shower and call it a night. I just came by to give you this letter. They delivered it to the house instead." Nate handed him a thick #9 envelope.

Glancing at it, Donovan forced himself not to react

when he saw the return address—Charlie Lincoln, Beaumont FCI. He stuffed it in his back pocket. "Thanks," he said as casually as he could. "I'll walk out with you."

Donovan braced for the questions, but either Nate didn't know FCI stood for Federal Correction Institute or he'd decided to mind his business. Either was good with Donovan.

"See ya around," Nate said, climbing on to his horse.

Donovan gave him a half wave and got into his truck.

Forcing himself to drive slowly, Donovan pulled down the long freshly paved driveway. He was deliberately not thinking about his father's letter or wondering how he had found him after all these years.

When he passed the ranch house, Emily came running off the porch to flag him down. He would have liked to hit the gas and leave her in a cloud of dust, but it was either deal with it now or deal with it later. With a sigh, he stopped and rolled down the window.

At least the view was good. She wore short cut-offs that showed her shapely legs and a tight pink cotton T-shirt. Her long blond hair was braided, but strands were flying around her face. She looked flushed and out of breath. His mind went straight to the gutter.

"Let me guess, you want to check my emissions to make sure the truck is compliant?" he drawled.

"Shit no. We're out of fireball and if I have to spend another minute in that house sober, someone isn't going to survive."

He grinned despite himself. "Hop in."

After climbing into the truck, she buckled up. He continued down the long driveway to the road. "What's going on?"

Emily sagged back in her seat and he noticed she had a spattering of freckles over her nose. She rolled her light blue eyes and made a face at him. "My father wants to ride out tomorrow morning—on a horse instead of in his truck. My mother is trying to talk some sense into him. Janice is throwing numbers and statistics at him about relapses and survivability of a third heart attack."

They passed by the rodeo school and saw Trent and Kelly taking pictures of their daughter, Alissa, riding a sheep and laughing.

"Traitors," Emily grumbled good-naturedly. "They bailed an hour ago."

Donovan had a momentary pang of jealousy for the happy family, before he stuffed that away. Trent was a good guy, and Kelly had always been nice to him. Their kid was cute as a button and he shouldn't begrudge them this time together.

But he did.

Because he never had anything like it. Family bonding time in the Lincoln family consisted of pickpocketing wallets during state fairs and rodeos, or running a con in out-of-town gas stations and shopping markets. Until, of course, it all went to shit.

"So, where to?" he asked.

"Where are you going?"

"The store to pick up some beer for this weekend. I could swing by the liquor store if you want."

"If you don't mind."

"I don't." There were worse ways to spend a Thursday night than with a pretty girl grabbing booze. Like reading a letter from his old man in prison.

"I was hoping to talk to you about your hunting excursions."

Then again…

"We've been through this," he said. "I thought we came to an understanding when the hogs chased you up a tree."

Emily sighed. "You seem like a really nice man."

"I'm not."

"My mom thinks so."

"I let her, so she saves me a piece of her apple pie."

"It is pretty good," Emily said. "I could bake you one."

"No thanks."

"Why not?"

"It would be the Trojan apple pie."

She giggled. "I don't know how that sounded in your head, but I'm picturing a pie full of condoms."

"You have issues," he said, but she had him smiling again.

"I have full-on anthologies." Emily sighed dramatically. "So would you, if you grew up with a father like I did."

"Yeah, you had it real bad." Had he managed to keep the bitterness out of his voice? Fuck it. He didn't care.

"I know you and my father have an agreement and that the rent you're paying is helping us keep the ranch. Of course, now with Trent coming into some money from riding Corazon del Diablo for eight seconds, we don't need a renter as much as we did before."

"Too bad. I have a three-year contract." It would take him half that to earn back his investment, but after three years, he should be able to leave the Three Sisters Ranch with a nice chunk of change. Any thought of staying permanently had fizzled as soon as he saw the letter from his father. If his father had managed to track him down, it was only a matter of time before other people did, too. Other people he'd spent a great deal of time avoiding. Samuel Barton came to mind.

Nope. Not going to go there. Damn, he hadn't let that name come into his head in a long time. That stupid letter was throwing him off his game and leaking into the protective walls he had put around off-limit thoughts.

He needed to get lost again—lost enough that his father couldn't find him.

Although, he was going to miss Emily Sullivan's bare legs. That was for damned sure.

"What if I had a business proposition that would be more lucrative than hunting?"

"You'd have better luck with another type of proposition," he said.

"Very funny."

"I wasn't joking."

"Anyway," she sighed in exasperation. "My father gave me sixty acres for my wind farm. I won't need all of that for the turbines, but that's the minimum we need to make sure the air flow currents aren't obstructed."

"What's that got to do with me?" He drove through the town of Last Stand and considered stopping at the Last

Stand Saloon for fireball shots and then finding out if Emily would taste like cinnamon when he kissed her. Donovan had already decided that if he was going to have to read the letter, he was going to treat himself. He couldn't think of a better treat than kissing Emily breathless.

"I'd like to make you a partner," she said, as if she was rolling out a grand adventure. Maybe to her, she was. "If you give up on your hunting business and invest in my wind turbines, I will cut you in on the profits once we lease the turbines out to the power companies."

Donovan wasn't a stranger to the long con or a short con, but maybe Emily really believed she was offering him a great deal. He decided to play along as they headed out of town to the H-E-B. "How much investment and how much profit?"

She leaned toward him eagerly and he fought to concentrate on the road. He was pretty sure she wasn't wearing a bra. "Janice ran the numbers for me. If we put up twenty turbines, we're looking at about a hundred and sixty thousand dollars a year. I want to put up at least fifty. But there's no way I'm going to get a loan for that amount. So my choices are to build this up piecemeal or get investors and do it at once for maximum profit."

He didn't know if he was offended that she considered him an easy mark or if she really believed the bullshit she was slinging. "You didn't answer my question," Donovan reminded her gently.

"The turbines are going to cost about forty grand each."

"You're not going to get a loan for much more than

that," he scoffed. "You'll pay it off in five years and then you'll have to start all over again with your second turbine."

"I was hoping you could buy in, fifty-fifty."

"For how long?"

"Forever. That's the beauty of getting in on the ground floor."

Those were terrible terms. For her. If he was a venture capitalist with a million dollars to invest, he'd jump all over that. Half of the profits in perpetuity? He'd make his money back in three years and then a two hundred thousand paycheck for the rest of his life. Shit yeah, he'd give up the hunting business for that kind of payday. There was only one problem.

"I don't have that kind of cash," he said regretfully.

His father could make it work. Or, at least, he could have convinced everyone involved that he did, back in his day. Of course, a lot of people would get hurt and lose their livelihoods and maybe even their lives.

"Shit," she said. "I was hoping to get you to buy one."

"You're thinking on a small scale. You want to find a Texas billionaire to partner up with. Not me."

"You know any?"

He used to. His father kept a notebook on all the whales, as he called them, with their weaknesses and net worth. If Barty Billionaire liked stacked blondes and had a weakness for betting on the long shot at the races, Donovan's father knew the best way to exploit it.

"No," Donovan said.

"Shit," she said again. "I thought I had a win-win situation here."

"I've already invested forty large into the hunting lodge and I need to have full hunting parties to make a profit. But once I do, I might take you up on that wind turbine action. Once my lease is up." It was an easy payday, and if he set it up so the money was wired into his account, his father couldn't use it to track him down. Even in jail, Charlie probably still had access to his vast network of contacts—to people who owed him favors. That was probably how he found him this time. Someone must have seen Donovan's hunting lodge advertisements or something and traded information with the old man.

"I'm surprised Nate isn't worried that your gun-toting clients will shoot the cattle." She crossed her arms in front of her.

"Probably because we're nowhere near the pasture lands. The land we hunt on isn't good for cattle. Not yet anyway."

He pulled into the liquor store parking lot. He was going to need something a little stronger than Ranger Creek beer if he was going to read the letter from his father. Of course, there was nothing saying he had to read it. He could toss it in the wood stove and pretend it never came. Although, Donovan figured it was better to read it and not be surprised if his father actually had something important to say. Like, he was being paroled and he'd be here next month. Suddenly, Donovan wanted nothing more than to read the letter, just on the appalling chance that's what it said.

Emily followed him into the store and wrinkled her nose at him when he picked out an expensive añejo tequila. "I can't drink that stuff."

"It's an acquired taste. You should come down to Mexico with me. I'd teach you to drink." Donovan was a little surprised that he meant it. He had a moment to fantasize about her in a string bikini drinking on a beach in Cozumel with him. Hell yeah.

"I know how to drink. Have you ever had *T'alla*?"

"Not that I'm aware of."

"Come to Ethiopia with me and I'll introduce you to it. It'll knock you on your ass."

"Sounds good to me. What is it?"

"It's a home-brewed beer. We can work you up to the *katikala*, which is a grain alcohol, about eighty-four proof."

"Even better." If his father was on his way, Ethiopia sounded like a good alternative. "Are there beaches in Ethiopia?"

She looked at him like he was stupid. "It's landlocked. The closest beach would be in the next country, over in Eritrea."

"Are they nice?"

"I heard they were. But it's almost impossible to get a visa to go there."

"Why?"

Emily shook her head. "It's a rough place."

"I'm surprised you didn't want to storm in there and push for life, liberty, and the pursuit of happiness."

She gave him a sad smile. "I'd never be seen again."

Sometimes, he forgot she wasn't the flighty wild child she pretended to be. "You've seen some shit," he said with growing respect.

"I saw a lot of great things, too. Have you ever been to Africa?"

"The farthest I've ever gone was Mexico on vacation and Canada for work."

"What did you do in Canada?"

"Hunt."

She made a face. What did she expect?

"So what else did you do in Africa, aside from drink?" he asked.

She pushed past him to go to the whiskey aisle. She took a bottle of fireball and a bottle of Jim Beam honey. "A lot. I was a community health volunteer. We did programs to educate the locals on sanitation, HIV and AIDS, malaria, those kinds of things. I especially liked working with the women in their gardens, though."

"Was it hard to be a vegetarian there?"

"Not really. I had to plan around some of the spicy meat stews. But there were a lot of lentil dishes and plenty of vegetables. I had *kinche* for breakfast, which is like oatmeal. It was harder being so far away from my family. Even though they drive me crazy, it was tough to live in a village, day in and day out, and see loving families without missing mine."

Donovan had no frame of reference on that, so he didn't say anything. To save himself a trip to the H-E-B, he grabbed a couple of cases of beer. If his hunters wanted anything else, they could order it or go out themselves.

"What about your family?" she asked as they were checking out.

"What about them?"

"Do you miss them?"

The question shouldn't be as complicated as it was. "My mother is dead."

"I'm so sorry," Emily said, her hand on her chest in shock.

"It was a long time ago."

"What about your dad?"

"I don't miss him at all."

Chapter Three

EMILY DIDN'T MEAN to drink so much fireball last night, but Donovan had plunked her back at home and her parents had still been arguing about her father's "lack of respect for the doctor's orders." So she locked herself in her room and drank alone, staring at the ceiling and trying not to think about Donovan Link.

They'd had a nice conversation that wasn't centered around both of them being adrenaline junkies. She would have liked to continue it, sipping fireball on his porch and enjoying the night. She thought she was really connecting with him on a personal level. She didn't want to be archenemies anymore. She liked their "dates" and how he made her feel when they talked about things that didn't make her want to scream in frustration. There had to be a way they could come to a compromise that didn't involve him killing animals on her family's land.

She should have asked to hang with him for a while and came back when her parents were asleep. But she had a feeling she would have wound up staying the night and that would have led to a complication she wasn't sure how to handle. Every time she looked into his gray eyes, she felt a sizzling connection she wanted to explore.

It wasn't that she hadn't thought about getting naked and sweaty with Donovan. But she was afraid he'd distract her from her mission to save the ranch. Now that she was back from Africa, she wanted to impress on her father and the rest of her family that she was ready for more responsibility.

Growing up, Emily and her sisters had gained experience taking care of the cattle and bringing them from pasture to pasture with the ranch hands. If she was the manager of the ranch, she wouldn't go out every day like her father did. That was Nate's and the ranch hands' area of expertise. She trusted Nate to handle that and bring any problems to her attention. Her father had the opposite opinion. He wanted to do everything, see everything, control everything. After almost forty years, it was now taking its toll. Once their finances were in order, she could concentrate on taking the reins from him and giving him the much-needed break he deserved.

And maybe then, they'd switch from beef cattle to milk cattle. Of course, there would be the added expense of building a dairy and surmounting a major learning curve, but that sort of thing excited her. Ideally, she wanted to get out of the cattle business entirely.

Like that would happen while her father had anything to say about it.

Emily needed to get her sisters on board with that first. Then they could work on their father together. Unfortunately, right now, they still considered her the baby of the family and indulged her wild ideas, but not one of them took her seriously. Once the wind turbines started bringing in profit, that would change. But damn, not today. Her head hurt too much and her mind was still too full of Donovan Link.

She stumbled down to breakfast, hungover and a little restless about her feelings for Donovan. Janice had cooked bacon and eggs for her parents. They were nowhere around, but the dishes were in the sink. Emily rinsed them off and put them in the dishwasher for her mother. Even after all these months back from Africa, she compared her host family's morning with these conveniences that she used to take for granted. She wondered how they were doing and decided she was going to write them a letter and get Kelly to give her some of the photos she'd taken of the ranch to send to them.

Reaching for the oatmeal, Emily made herself a big bowl, and cut up a banana and added it in along with a handful of walnuts. After her second cup of coffee, she started feeling human again.

Her mother walked in and did a double take. "Weren't you supposed to meet with Kendrick at the bank this morning?"

Adrenaline shot through Emily. "Oh shit, that was today?" A quick glance at her phone told her she had fifteen minutes to get there. It was a ten-minute trip.

"Oh, Emily," her mother sighed.

Ignoring that, Emily ran upstairs and tossed off her pajamas. Grabbing a sundress, she slithered into it and roughly ran a brush through her long hair.

"I should just cut it all off," she muttered, wincing at the snarls as her fingers flew, putting it into a messy braid. Slipping on sandals, she grabbed her purse and sprinted outside. There wasn't a car she could take.

"Not today," she groaned, dialing Kelly's number.

Her oldest sister didn't answer her phone. Janice, however, answered on the second ring.

"Can you take me into town or can I borrow your car? I'm late for my bank appointment."

"I'm sorry, Emily. I'm going to need my car this afternoon."

"That's okay. Just drop me off at the bank and I'll call an Uber or something to come back. I just can't wait for one now."

"All right, I'll be right there."

Janice sounded aggravated, and Emily couldn't blame her. She should have made arrangements for a car last night. Her only excuse was she'd been distracted by her parents' argument and her solitary drinking.

In a weird way, things had been so much easier in Africa. The pace was slower and the day was all about the people and the village. There weren't strangers coming in and hunting on their lands, and there was no rushing to the bank or the liquor store. Even though she had been back for months, there were moments—before sleep fully faded—when Emily thought she was back in her host family's hut.

Then she felt relieved and a little guilty when she realized that she was in her comfortable bed instead of her sleeping bag on the floor, and remembered that she could take a long, hot shower and then go downstairs and have plenty to eat.

Did her parents really need her more than her friends in West Tigray? After all, Trent had taken some of the pressure off them by buying the land instead of leasing it, so he now owned the land his school and the house he was building were on. Donovan wasn't going anywhere for the next few years. And Janice's retreat was about to go live. Emily was reasonably sure she could go back to Ethiopia and finish out her contract and nobody would miss her. Or she could even sign up for a two-year tour. It would take her to another place, but she could help people who desperately needed it. Her parents' situation wasn't as dire as her father's message had made out.

Did they even need her? She'd been hoping to impress them with her traveling and missionary work. And while Emily thought they were proud of her, she still didn't believe they thought of her as anything other than "the baby."

But that was a cop-out. They weren't expecting anything to come of her plans, because nothing ever had. This time, she was going to prove them wrong.

Of course, not being late to this important meeting would go a long way to convincing her parents she was more responsible.

Janice barely stopped the car long enough for her to jump in before tearing down the driveway.

"What's the rush?"

"I have to be back in time for the plumber. Look, I don't want you to be disappointed when Kendrick turns you down for the loan."

"Whoa, nice way to be supportive." Emily crossed her arms over her chest.

"They turned Kelly down and she had a job."

"I have a stipend from the Peace Corps."

"It's not enough."

"And money in the bank," Emily challenged.

"So did Kelly."

"I could use the land as collateral."

"It's not your land to do that."

"Dad gave it to me."

"There is no deed. He's letting you use it, but it's still legally his. At the very least, they're going to ask for a cosigner for the loan. You can't get Mom or Dad to do it because they're mortgaged to the hilt."

"Hey, Nancy Negative, knock it off. I got this." OMG, could Janice get any bossier?

Janice sighed. "I just don't want you to be crushed when this falls apart. It means the world to Dad that you came home when he needed you. That's enough for us."

Emily tried not to let Janice see how much her words hurt her. They were totally expecting her to fuck this up. Well, that wasn't going to happen. She refused to talk to Janice the rest of the way to town. She forced herself not to slam the car door.

Taking a few deep breaths, she steadied herself and straightened her shoulders. She was going to show them all.

IT TOOK LESS than fifteen minutes.

The answer wasn't just no. It pretty much had been hell no. Emily managed not to cry until she left the bank and then she ripped the elastic tie from her hair so she could hide her face as the tears streamed down. She had been so sure she could convince the bank it was easy money. And it was. Once the turbines were built, they would start generating profit.

Scrubbing her face, she looked up and saw Donovan staring at her from across the street. He was coming out of the post office and was now walking toward her. Crap, she had to get herself under control. Emily ducked down an alley and ran to the end. She didn't want to see him while she felt so raw. After darting into the hardware store through the back door, she walked down to where they kept the washers and dryers and pretended to read the energy readouts on them until she could breathe without hiccupping. She smoothed her hair back from her face and put it back into a messy ponytail. When she turned to go, she found Donovan leaning up against the wall.

"How did you find me?"

"I'm used to tracking elusive prey."

"Great. Does that mean you're going to shoot me?" It would be the highlight of her day.

"I was hoping to take you to lunch."

Emily thought about it. "Okay."

He slung his arm around her and walked with her back to his truck. She was startled at first. Why was her stomach hurtling like they were zipping over a ravine? Donovan smelled like leather and pine and it made her toes curl. She wanted to rub her cheek against his soft shirt. He felt comforting and solid and she needed that right now.

"What were you doing in town?" she asked.

He tensed briefly and then relaxed. "I had to send something. How about you?"

"I had my meeting with the loan officer. I thought since he went to high school with my sister and since the wind turbines were a sure fucking thing, I'd get a big fat loan. I got a big fat nothing instead."

"I'm sorry," he said.

Emily was grateful that he didn't follow it up with "I told you so" or "What did you expect?"—which was what she was going to get when she went home. They drove out of town for a bit and she was beginning to wonder where he was taking her. Not that she cared. It was nice to go for a drive in the quiet. Her parents weren't arguing about her father pushing himself too hard. Janice wasn't lecturing, and Trent and Kelly weren't all lovey-dovey.

If she was with anyone other than Donovan, she would have called it peaceful. Donovan made her feel restless and a little wild, like they were hurtling out of an airplane. Emily had left her wild side here in Last Stand when she went off to Africa. She was surprised that it was right here waiting for her. The wildness in her lived for zip-lining across ravines, riding Janice's racehorse at top speed down the trails leading to the cow pastures, and seeing how close she could get to Donovan without giving in to the desire to kiss him.

He pulled down a hidden side street and they bounced

along an unpaved drive until they came to a cute little diner. Donovan's was the only car in the small parking lot. The sign outside proclaimed it as the Mustard Seed.

"What's this?"

"Lunch." He went around and opened the car door for her.

"You're being awfully nice," she said suspiciously.

"Don't get used to it," he said.

"Hi, welcome to the Mustard Seed," a young woman said as they came in. "My name's Carrie. I'll be your waitress. We just opened for business today and you're our first customers. So drinks are on the house. What can I get you?"

"Trust me?" Donovan asked.

"Sure," Emily said, wondering what he was up to. She accepted a menu from Carrie.

"Oktoberfest for me, and she'll have the Paleta de Mango."

"Sounds good," Carrie said and walked in the back.

"What is that? And how did you know about this place?" Emily looked at the menu hoping to find a decent salad and stared in disbelief. "This is a vegetarian restaurant."

"One of my hunters from last week mentioned his sister's place was opening today and I figured you'd like to go."

Now she felt like crying for a different reason. "Thanks. I really needed this today."

Carrie came back with two frothy beers in large pint glasses with the name Rahr & Sons etched on them. "I'll give you a few minutes with the menu, but I have a few specials as well. Would you like to hear them?"

Emily nodded vigorously.

"We've got a zucchini po' boy served with sweet potato fries for ten ninety-nine, and our cashew and quinoa burger patty served with seitan fakin' bacon, soy cheese, and the works on a sesame seed bun. It comes with a side of onion rings for twelve ninety-nine."

Emily wanted both. Plus the carrot ginger soup and the buffalo chik'n nachos. "Do you deliver?" she asked instead.

Carrie laughed. "No, ma'am, not yet."

"Can I live here?" Emily grinned.

"I might have a waitress position open," Carrie joked. "To handle the lunch crowd." She gestured to the nearly empty restaurant.

Emily was considering it, especially if meals were included.

"I'll have the grilled portabella quesadilla," Donovan said. "You want to split the nachos?"

"You're damned right I want to split the nachos." Emily nodded. "I'll get the zucchini po' boy for here and the cashew quinoa special to go."

"You got it," Carrie said and went back to the kitchen.

"Don't worry," Emily said. "I'll pay."

"I'm not worried. And you're not paying," Donovan said mildly.

Emily was going to protest, but saw the look in his eyes. She was used to his stubbornness by now. "All right," she said. "But I'll pay next time."

"No, you won't." He relented and smiled at her, though.

She took a deep slug of her beer and gasped in surprise.

Paleta de Mango apparently was a mango chili beer with lime. It was wonderful, but spicy and not at all what she expected. She grabbed Donovan's Oktoberfest and drank half of it to cleanse her palate.

"I wasn't expecting that."

"I wasn't either," he said ruefully, finishing off what was left of his beer.

"It's different. Now that I know what it's supposed to taste like, I'll be fine."

Carrie brought them over refills with the nachos and Emily began to relax. "I don't usually drink so much, but it's been a tough week."

"Amen," Donovan said, and clicked her glass. "Do you have a plan about what you're going to do next?"

"Way to harsh my buzz, man," she said.

"Sorry."

"I've been racking my brain and the only person I know who's close to being a billionaire is Trent. I know he won that three-million-dollar purse, but I feel weird asking him for money. He's already bailed us out once. Although at this point, I'm ready to take Carrie up on her offer. One of the biggest problems the bank had was my lack of employment."

"You should ask Trent. What's the worst he could say?"

Emily could think of a bunch of nasty things her father would say, but Trent was not her father. "I guess. If he says no, I'm no worse off. But then what?"

"You'll figure something out."

Emily had to take a sip of her beer so he didn't see how much his words affected her. Her family would have never said that. They would have given her constructive criticism instead, telling her what she did wrong.

"I'm not out of ideas yet. I've got a lead from a friend of mine in the Peace Corps. It's his brother-in-law's best friend kind of deal."

Donovan's eyes narrowed. "What kind of deal?"

"Don't know yet. I've got to call the number and see what he has to say."

"Well, just be careful. There are a lot of con artists out there looking to rook an innocent mark."

"I'm not an innocent mark." Now he was beginning to sound like her family. And it had all been going so well.

He tried to hide his scoff and it pissed her off. But then her zucchini po' boys came and they were fried crispy balls of perfection, and she pretended he didn't exist.

Chapter Four

DONOVAN CUT HIMSELF off at two beers, even though he could drink Rahrs all day with Emily. He had to drive them home safely, so he enjoyed watching her face as she ate with gusto. It was worth giving up a venison burger or barbecue ribs to take her here. And the food was really good. Next time he talked to Jimmy, he'd let him know that they ate at his sister's place and would probably be coming back.

Spending time with Emily was taking his mind off his father. As usual, he was asking for forgiveness and money in the same letter. He gave him the latter, but would never give him the former. How the old fool had tracked him down was beyond him. Donovan had changed his name from Lincoln to Link after his mother's death and his father's imprisonment. He had moved all over Texas and never once left a forwarding address. Still, Charlie Lincoln had contacts and Donovan had stopped moving long enough to be traceable. Now that Charlie knew Donovan was taking wealthy hunters on gaming weekends, it was only a matter of time before he got another letter concerning a "business proposition" he had thought up. Although unlike Emily's earnest proposition, Charlie would want to fleece the hunters for all that he could.

He pushed thoughts of his father out of his mind. The money Donovan sent to shut him up should keep him out of his hair for a few more months. It might be worth it to set him up with monthly contributions into his prison account, as long as Donovan made it clear the payments stopped if he got another letter. That sounded like a plan. He smiled in relief that he'd thought of it.

"We should be getting back to the ranch," Emily said reluctantly when Carrie brought her the to-go meal and the check for him.

"Why?" he asked. Mexico still seemed like a good idea to him.

"Well, you have hunters coming in tonight and I need to talk to Trent."

"Okay," he said good-naturedly and stretched. He gave a mental check that he was all right to drive and then paid the bill and tip in cash. Donovan slung his arm around her again because she felt so damn good next to him and they walked back out to his truck.

"Are you going to behave yourself this weekend?" he asked as he started up the car.

"Was that what this was about? A bribe to keep me docile?"

He snorted. "Is that all it would have taken?"

"The food is amazing, but it wasn't that amazing." She sighed. "I really hate that you kill animals for sport. It enrages me that you make money off it. And it makes me cry that you're doing it on my family's property."

"With your father's permission and hearty approval," he said, feeling he had to point out the obvious, even though it sounded defensive to his ears.

"And the fact that there's nothing I can do to stop you makes it even worse."

"You can't always get what you want," he said.

"I know that."

He thought she might be pouting, so he threw her a bone. "I'm not going to renew the lease after the three years are up."

"You're going to up and leave? What about your building?"

"Your father or Trent will compensate me as per my rental agreement. I had the option to continue to rent or buy the land."

"My father was going to sell you that land?"

Her shocked response showed him that she hadn't been aware of that.

"It would have all been legal and wouldn't have encroached on the cattle pastures. But don't worry. I'm going to make some money and get the hell out."

She was silent for such a long time, he thought she was in a food coma and then she said in a small, hurt voice, "Is it because of me?"

"What?" He took his eyes off the road to stare at her. She was serious. "No. It'll just be time to move on." Maybe leave Texas for good. See how good his father's contacts really were. Would they be able to follow him to California or

Montana? Would he have to leave the country to finally get rid of him? "I don't stay in one place for very long." He had thought the Three Sisters Ranch would be different, but even if it was, Donovan couldn't risk having his father show up one day. He'd claim to be all rehabilitated after fifteen years in prison.

Donovan didn't want the stigma of being Charlie Lincoln's son to taint whatever legitimate business Donovan decided to get involved with. Charlie was a grifter and Donovan didn't dare trust a word he said. It was better to pretend his father had died with his mother.

Rehabilitated my ass.

"Then there's no reason to fight anymore, then. Not if you're leaving anyway."

"Nope," he agreed. "You just have to deal with me for another few years and then I'll leave you and your family's ranch in my rear mirror."

"Where will you go?"

He shrugged. "I'll figure something out."

"Do you think you'll ever settle down?"

"Maybe." He didn't like how serious this conversation was turning. "How about you? After you set up your wind turbine farm, are you heading back to Ethiopia?"

"No. I did good work and I'm proud of what I did. But it's nice to have all the modern conveniences that I took for granted before living in Ethiopia for three years. Running water. Clean water. The internet. Sometimes I think I'm a sellout. Other times I tell myself it's time to grow up and start a career."

"Like waitressing in a vegetarian restaurant?"

"I was thinking ranch owner."

Donovan loved her enthusiasm. "Good for you."

"Did you always want to be a hunter?"

"Nah, I wanted to be a cowboy."

"Why aren't you?"

Good question. "My parents had other plans." Why was he going down this road?

"Did they want you to be a doctor or something else more white-collar?"

That would work as an answer. "Yeah, something like that." They were hoping for the big score, so they'd be able to move down to Fiji or Tahiti and live out the rest of their lives on the beach. Like that would have satisfied them. They'd be back to rooking the locals within a year.

"You could still be a cowboy," she said. "You don't have to go. You could stay and just not shoot things."

"Sweetheart, are you asking me to stay?" he teased.

"Yes."

That stopped him in his tracks. "Why? I thought we were adversaries."

"We won't be, once you stop killing animals."

"Thanks, no one has ever asked me to stay before." It gave him a warm feeling that he didn't want to trust.

"So are you going to stay?"

"I'll tell you in three years," he said. Hopefully his father wouldn't make it sooner.

When they pulled into the Three Sisters Ranch, Donovan parked in Trent's lot. "I don't think he's home."

"Maybe he took Kelly and Alissa out," she said. "Let's go look around."

The studio was locked, but they checked out the barn just to make sure. "Just horse shit and sheep shit," Donovan said.

"Let's see if they're at the new house," she said, tangling her fingers through his as they walked back to the house that was in the final stages of development. He had work to do, but for the moment he wanted to be with Emily.

"Hello," she called, walking up the unfinished stairs. There wasn't even a door.

"Big house," he commented, looking around at the construction that was nearing completion.

"Alissa is so excited she gets her own room."

The floors were finished, but the walls were only half sheet-rocked. They looked around, but it was clear no one was around.

"Oh well, I'll have to catch up with him later." Emily put her hands on her hips and let out a breath. "I guess I delayed the inevitable as long as I could. I've got to go home and face my failure."

"It's not a failure. It's just a bump in the road."

She reached for his hand again. "I don't suppose you could come with me as a buffer."

"I'm not sure what type of buffer I'd be, but I can give you a few more hours. Then I've got to do an equipment check."

"You mean clean and load the rifles." Emily dropped his hand.

"No, they're bringing their own rifles. I need to make sure we have the gear to camp out in and to check that they all emailed me copies of their licenses."

"Don't you think they'd rather do trail riding?" she asked hopefully, a sweet, wistful look on her face.

"No, I do not." He hoped she wasn't starting this shit again. He really thought they had made some progress today.

To his surprise, she left it at that. As they were walking out of the house, she turned back to him. "I had a really nice time today. Thanks."

"I wouldn't mind doing it again," he said.

Standing up on her tiptoes, she gave him a real kiss. Pressing herself up against him, she slid her arms around his neck and opened her mouth under his.

Hell. He hadn't expected that.

Donovan staggered back from the punch of desire that hit him low and hard. Crushing her to him, he took her sweet mouth and everything else she was offering. He was damned sure she wasn't wearing a bra under her sundress and he was damned tempted to slide it down to find out. A part of him was dimly aware they were kissing in the middle of her sister's house that had no freaking door, but he couldn't stop. Not when she felt so sweet and right in his arms. It was like kissing an angel in sunshine.

Emily made little needy noises in her throat that were driving him wild. Reaching down, he cupped her ass and held her against his cock that was pressing tight against his jeans. Her fingers tangled in his hair as she reached up to kiss him deeper. He tugged her dress down to her waist and her breasts popped free. Kissing down her neck, Donovan thumbed a taut nipple as she gasped and wiggled. The rest of her dress slid to the floor. As he sucked on one rosy tip and then the other, she spread her legs when he dipped his hand inside her tiny panties.

She held his head to her breast, and cried out in pleasure when he rubbed his finger across her wet slit and then fingered her fast.

"Please," she choked out, but his mouth was too full to ask what she was begging for.

Donovan flicked his fingers over her tight bud as he kissed back up her chest to take her hot mouth with his again. Clutching his shoulders, her moans were muffled as he brought her trembling body closer to orgasm. Emily undulated on his fingers, her willing body letting him do whatever he wanted.

When she stiffened, he wrapped his hand around her ponytail and pulled her hair back so he could watch her come apart in his arms. Her eyes wide and her mouth open and gasping, Emily pressed her thighs together on his hand as she rode out the tremors.

"I can't believe that just happened," she said shakily, as her eyes refocused.

"You and me both, sweetheart. But I want to do it again."

"Donovan?" Trent called from outside.

"Oh shit," they both said at the same time and banged heads as they both bent down for her dress.

"Stall him," she hissed, pushing him toward the open

doorway.

Donovan staggered, rubbing his forehead. His body was still screaming for him to bury himself in Emily's hot wetness. Adjusting himself the best he could, he walked out the door and blocked Trent just as he was coming up the stairs.

"Hey, buddy." Donovan clapped him on the arm and steered him away from the door. "Looks good. You should be getting the certificate of occupancy soon, right?"

"Yeah, what are you doing around here?"

Emily popped out. "He drove me home. I was looking for you. I need to talk to you about something."

Donovan gave her a quick once-over. Aside from her nipples clearly outlined against her sundress, she didn't look as if they'd been screwing around. He side-eyed Trent, but the guy didn't seem to notice his soon-to-be sister-in-law was braless.

"I'll see you later, Donovan." Emily smiled at him.

Donovan wasn't sure what that meant, but it was a damned uncomfortable walk back to his truck.

Chapter Five

ADRENALINE WAS STILL racing through Emily. Her heart was pounding, but her legs felt like jelly. The last thing she wanted to do right now was talk business with Trent. No, she wanted to follow Donovan back to his hunting lodge and finish in his bed what they'd started. Emily was so glad she had finally kissed him properly. If she'd waited around for him to do it, it could have taken until his lease was up. Now that she knew she would only have to deal with the hunters crawling all over her family's ranch for a few more years, it was bearable. Donovan was bearable and they could have fun.

She missed having fun.

As she sat across the desk from Trent, she tried not to blush because if Trent been five minutes earlier, he would have gotten an eyeful. It could have been much worse, though. Her father could have been with him.

Things were still pretty tense between Trent and her dad. Trent was Alissa's father, which had been an almost six-year mystery to everyone except Kelly. Her father, to put it mildly, lost his mind when he found out. Emily wasn't sure what to think. At first, she blamed Trent. But then she realized he hadn't known about Alissa. If he had, he would have moved heaven and earth to be with Kelly and his daughter.

And now that he was going to marry her sister, her father was just going to have to make peace with him. But Frank Sullivan wasn't known for his forgiving nature. Luckily, Trent didn't hold a grudge. Still, it was going to be awkward to ask him to invest in her wind turbines. He had already done so much for the Three Sisters Ranch. He'd used his purse from riding a devil bull that nearly crippled him the first time, and almost killed him the second time, to buy the land that had his school and this new house on outright.

"What can I do for you, Emily?" he asked as they walked back to his rodeo school where he, Kelly, and Alissa were living until the house was finished.

"Where's my sister?"

"Alissa had a playdate with someone she met at the Y during her swimming lessons. They should be back by dinner."

"That's good. I actually wanted to talk to you alone." She didn't want Trent to feel obligated to help her if he didn't really want to. It was easier for him to say no if Kelly wasn't there pressuring him to say yes. Emily followed him into the school and into his office. Trent pulled a water out of his fridge and offered her one. Crap, she left her veggie burger in Donovan's truck. Oh well, that would just give her an excuse to go pick it up later. She accepted the water and took a deep drink. Her throat was dry from all that gasping and moaning. So much for not complicating things by having hot, sweaty sex with Donovan. Now that was going to be all she thought of. Well, that and the wind turbines.

"What can I do for you?" Trent eased himself into his chair and propped his bad leg up on a padded stool, wincing.

"You all right?"

"Just a little stiff."

He would never admit to being in pain. "I went to the bank today. They turned me down for a loan."

"Why?"

She blinked at the interruption. She was expecting him to say he was sorry or not say anything. "Well, while they thought it would be a good investment, they didn't have a lot of confidence in me."

"They don't know you well, do they?" Trent smiled at her.

If he could only convince her parents of that.

"They thought I was too young. I don't have a credit history."

He snorted. "You'd think that was a good thing. No credit card debt or existing loans."

Emily felt her mood lighten a bit. "Right? Well, in addition to that, they didn't count the Peace Corps as viable work experience. So I was shit out of luck." She paused, gathering her nerve. "Would you be interested in being my partner for the wind turbines?" Emily blurted, leaning forward in her chair. She was eager to get her pitch out before he could say no. "Fifty-fifty split. Of course, you'd have to front all the money." Hell, that sounded terrible even to her ears. This was a long shot. She didn't bring anything to the table on this deal, except for the land and that wasn't even hers.

This was a disaster. No wonder the bank turned her down.

"How much do you want?" he asked.

Emily's mouth dropped open and she sat stunned for a moment. "How much you got?" she said after she recovered. "The wind turbines are about forty thousand each. And they'll return that investment in about five years."

"How much do you have?"

She puffed out a humorless laugh. "Not enough."

"I've got an idea," he said. "I'm not sure you're going to like it."

"Hit me with it," Emily said. "You're my last hope."

"Kelly wants to take photographs. Janice is into her horse therapy business. And Frank isn't getting any younger. I know it would ease his mind if one of the three of you were interested in ranching."

"I'd love to run this ranch, but I don't have the experience to claim being a manager. That was part of the problem the bank had."

"I'll loan you some money. I don't want to go into business with you because I don't want Frank to think I'm trying to take over the ranch one sister at a time. I also don't feel right making a profit from the loan. So instead, I want you to make training to take over the ranch your job."

That sounded too good to be true. "What's the catch?"

"The catch is you have to convince your father that you're the heir apparent. And that means you need to convince your sisters, get Nate on board, and ease any doubts in your parents' minds that you can handle the responsibility."

For a minute, she had been afraid he was going to tell her the condition of the loan was that they had to keep raising beef cattle to slaughter. "I can do that," she said quickly, before he changed his mind on the terms. "But I want to get at least ten turbines. Are you in for a half a million?"

Trent choked on his water.

She knew his purse from riding Corazon del Diablo was close to three million. But she also knew he'd spent a lot already, buying the land for his house and school from her father. Not to mention building his new house and putting money into his business. Plus, he was planning a wedding and there was also Alissa's college fund to think about. Emily blew out a nervous sigh. "Of course, anything you can give me, I would be appreciative."

"I was thinking about half that," Trent said.

Emily couldn't keep the grin off her face. "I won't let you down."

"I know. Look, Kelly is really worried about your dad. If you can get him to retire by taking on his duties, it'll be completely worth loaning you the money."

"You're a good man, Trent. Especially since my dad has been a bit of a jerk to you."

"He's my daughter's grandfather. He doesn't have to treat me like a son. As long as Alissa is the apple of his eye, he's all right in my book."

"Are you kidding me?" Emily smiled. "She had him attending a tea party with her action figures the other day."

Nodding, Trent returned her smile. "That's what I want for him. For both of them. With you and Nate working together, the Three Sisters Ranch will come back better than ever."

Except for that pesky cow-murdering thing. But one battle at a time. Still, her conscience nudged her to let Trent know about her plans. She took in a deep breath. "I have some major changes I want to make to the ranch."

"That's between you and your sisters. And after Frank's retired." Trent clamped his hands over his ears playfully. "Start off with the wind turbines and take it from there."

She stood up and put out her hand. "I appreciate the confidence you're placing in me."

"Why wouldn't I be confident in you? You basically ran a ranch in Ethiopia."

"Not even close. But I get what you're saying. I've got transferable skills. I wish the bank had seen that." She wished her family could see it.

"More importantly, you have the drive and determination to make this work."

They hammered out the details for the next half hour or so and Emily left feeling confident and in control of her life for the first time in...well, ever.

DINNER THAT NIGHT was painful. Only her parents, Nate, and Janice were at the table. Her mom had made fried chicken, mashed potatoes, and some corn that they had canned from the summer crops. Emily substituted vegetarian chicken nuggets and tried not to feel like she was eating a kiddie meal.

"How did everything go at the bank?" her father said as soon as her mother got done pouring them all iced tea.

"Dad," Janice said with a resigned sigh. "We don't have to talk about this at the dinner table."

"It's okay," Emily said, reaching for a snowflake roll. "I got turned down for the loan."

Janice looked at her plate. Her parents exchanged knowing glances, but Nate said, "I'm sorry to hear that, Emily. I know you had your heart set on the wind turbines."

"I do, but don't worry. They're still going through."

"How?" her father asked scornfully.

"I have some contacts from the Peace Corps who can help me out. And in the meantime, Trent loaned me some money."

Frank dug into his chicken angrily. He probably should be eating grilled chicken instead of chicken that had been buttermilk-dipped and fried in her mother's special crushed corn flake and potato chip coating. And the butter and gravy drenching his mashed potatoes weren't such a good idea either. But there was no telling him that. At least he was putting some weight on again.

"We can't expect Trent to give us a handout every time we ask," he said. "He put his body on the line for that money and he's still paying for that decision."

"Careful, Dad. It's beginning to sound like you've forgiven him," Janice said, trying to lighten the mood.

"I'll like him better once he puts a ring on Kelly's finger."

"June will be here before you know it," Janice said.

"I'm not wearing a monkey suit."

Emily and Janice shared an amused glance. He'd wear a tuxedo if his granddaughter asked him to.

"And you better not piss away Trent's money."

"I'll be paying Trent back as soon as I can. This is a loan. Not a handout," Emily said, trying to keep her voice light and even. "The wind turbines will make us about eight thousand dollars a year. I should be able to pay Trent back in a little under six years."

"That's if all you do with the profits is pay him back. It may be longer than that," Janice broke in. "Is Trent all right with waiting?"

Trying not to grind her teeth in frustration, Emily gave her sister a sharp nod. Trent said to take ten years, but Emily was determined to get rid of the loan as soon as possible.

"It's a big responsibility," her mother said. "Are you sure you know what you're doing?"

"Yes," Emily said. Short and sweet and to the point. "But speaking of responsibility, now that I'm back home for good and I've got those wind turbines coming in, it's time for me to get more serious about learning how to manage the ranch. And you should be getting serious about retiring."

Janice dropped her fork. It was loud in the sudden silence. Nate gave Emily a "What are you doing?" look.

"What the hell does that mean?" Frank said with his

mouth full.

Her mother put her hand on his arm. "I'd be happy to show you the books, Emily. It will be good to have a second eye on things."

"I think it's the next logical step. After all, Janice is going to have her hands full with the retreat center."

Frank snorted.

Janice clenched her jaw.

"I don't know anyone who is going to want to pay to camp out on our land," Frank growled.

"It's a good thing you're not my demographic, then," Janice said with fake sweetness.

Emily jumped in before they could get into a heated discussion. "And Kelly is going to be busy with her portrait studio and helping Trent with his bull-riding school."

"So?" Frank said, reaching for another dollop of mashed potatoes.

"So that leaves me to become your successor."

"What about Nate here?" Frank jerked a thumb at Nate, who had a chicken leg halfway up to his mouth.

"Please don't get me involved with this. I'm the foreman. If I wanted to manage a ranch, I would have wasted my money going to college."

"He doesn't want it," Janice said.

"That's what he just said." Emily rolled her eyes at her sister. "Anyway, that leaves me to be your second-in-command, Daddy. I'm going to be your shadow. I'll be going with you on the cattle drives in the morning and learning everything else from you and Nate. That way, when you're ready to retire, the transition will be seamless."

"Retire? I'm not ready to retire."

"Maybe we're ready," Janice muttered.

Emily kicked her under the table. "What Janice means is that we're worried about your health."

"Save your worries. I'll be fine."

"Yes, but you've worked so hard all your life. And you made sure we had the best of everything."

Janice looked down at her plate. "That's right."

"We want you to take time to enjoy the little things, like Alissa and going fishing in the pond. Relax more and maybe even take Mom on a vacation."

Nate might have muttered something that sounded like "that'll be the day," but Janice gave him a sharp elbow.

"Amen to that," Sarah said.

"I can't leave the ranch," Frank said halfheartedly. She was getting through to him. "I've taken off so much time already, being in the hospital."

"Sure you can," Nate said. "We've got this."

Emily held her father's gaze waiting to see what he was going to lob out next, but to her surprise he just grunted and went back to eating. "I would like to go out with Donovan and bag some deer."

Emily closed her eyes in frustration. One thing at a time.

"You do know we leave before five in the morning," Nate said. "Cows got to be fed."

"I am aware of that." Like she hadn't spent most of her summers on horseback with the ranch hands going from pasture to pasture and rounding up the cattle. "But there's a lot more that I should be involved in, like the welfare of the cattle." And eventually getting them out of the meat business entirely, but that was a discussion for another day.

Baby steps.

"Glad to see someone is going to use their college degree to help with the ranch," her father said with a pointed look at Janice. And just like that, Emily was off the hook. She had never been happier for her animal science degree.

Janice was a veterinary technician who left the ranch to work with horses in dressage farms. Her father was still holding a grudge about that. Janice flipped her the bird under the table, but Emily felt vindicated since Janice had been an unbearable pill to her this morning. She knew her sisters loved her, but there were times when they got on each other's nerves.

Her mother served an apple pie for dessert, which her father probably shouldn't be eating either.

"I'm going to take Donovan a piece," she said, rising up from the table.

Her father gaped at her for a moment, but recovered quickly. "I thought I told you to leave him alone."

"You told me to stop pestering him. I don't think bringing him a slice of homemade apple pie qualifies, do you?"

Narrowing his eyes at her, he said, "What are you up to? You're not going to doctor the pie so he gets the shits tomorrow and can't lead the hunt?"

"Dad," Janice said, exasperatedly.

"I hadn't thought of that. That's a good one, Dad. No, he took me out to lunch this afternoon and I thought this might be a nice thank-you."

"You went out on a date with Donovan Link?" Janice said.

"It was lunch."

Her mother and father exchanged a look, and he shrugged. "Ask him if he's seen Ghost yet."

"I damn well will not," Emily said. She wasn't going to mention the white elk to a trophy hunter. That was all they needed—to have every yahoo with a rifle shooting at flashes of white for the chance to cut off and mount the head in their living room.

"Kelly wants to take some pictures of her," Janice said. "Donovan knows not to shoot her. We want him to track her. Kelly is planning on entering the pictures in the state fair next year. It would be great publicity for the ranch."

And for Donovan's hunting tours, Emily thought sourly.

After wrapping a large slice of pie, Emily went outside. It was a nice night for a ride and she was going to stay on the new paved road, which was well lit, so she saddled Sunflower up and headed over. Unfortunately, there were several cars in his parking lot and the entire hunting lodge had every light on.

"Oh shit," she said. His hunting party had already arrived.

"Hey, who's this?" one of the men said from the porch as she approached. Sunflower flicked an ear, but otherwise didn't respond.

"I'm here to see Donovan," she said, getting down from her horse. She securely tied her to the hitching post outside because Sunflower had a habit of untying herself and wandering back to the barn.

"Hey, Donny, your girl is here," another called back into the hunting lodge.

She climbed the stairs and they parted. Two of them smiled down at her and the others couldn't be bothered.

"Hey," Donovan said, coming out of the lodge. She was relieved he was here. The hunters were giving off some crazy vibes. You could almost taste the testosterone.

"I'm sorry to bother you. I wanted to swap my burger for a slice of Mom's apple pie."

"Come on in," he said. "Guys, make yourselves at home. There's more beer in the fridge and I think there's a football game on in the basement on the wide screen."

A few of the hunters decided to finish their cigarettes, but the others wandered back inside. Donovan led her into his office and shut the door.

"I love the smell of toxic masculinity in the evening," Emily said.

He went into a mini-fridge and handed her the bag from the Mustard Seed. She exchanged it for the apple pie. "You didn't have to come all the way out here tonight. I would have dropped off your lunch before we left tomorrow morning."

"I didn't come here for just for that. I didn't think your hunters were coming until later."

"They made good time. So why did you come?" He crossed his arms over his chest. "You're not here to cause trouble, are you?"

Emily flicked the lock on his office door. "It depends on how you define trouble." She kicked off her shoes. Her nipples puckered in anticipation as she pulled the T-shirt she had changed into over her head.

"Christ, woman, don't you ever wear a bra?"

"Bitch, bitch, bitch," she said, unbuttoning her jeans and sliding them and her panties down.

Donovan's eyes went wide. "I don't know what the hell those guys were smoking out there, but if this is a hallucination, I'm going to empty my bank account to buy some more."

"We got interrupted before. I wasn't finished yet." She walked into his arms. His hands were everywhere. They were rough against her soft skin, but it made her want to purr like a cat.

"Are you fucking serious?" he said. "I've got a house full of riled-up men."

"They're watching Texas A&M downstairs." She tugged his T-shirt out of his pants and slid her palms up over his chest.

"I can't be away for long," he groaned. "I want to take my time with you."

"I don't want it slow, Donovan," she said, unsnapping his pants and pulling down his zipper.

When she reached inside his briefs, he took in a sharp breath and said, "All right, have it your way." He picked her up and slung her over his shoulder. She managed not to shriek as he opened a door in the back of his office and strode through it. Emily saw it was a cozy bedroom before she was dumped on his bed.

"I brought condoms," she said, suddenly breathless as he shed his clothes. "They're in my jeans pocket."

He looked great naked, his biceps and abs clearly defined. Emily couldn't wait to have him next to her. He opened up the drawer in his bedside table, tossed a few on the bed, and then covered his body with hers.

"Finally," she groaned, wrapping a leg around his. He was hot and hard, the wiry hairs on his leg coarse and satisfying against her skin.

Then he was kissing her and she got lost in the sweet slide of their bodies and his hot mouth plundering hers. Reaching down between them, Emily wrapped her hand around his cock and tugged on it with slow pulls. Now it was his turn to moan into her mouth. When the thrusting and rubbing built to a fever pitch, she tore open a condom and slipped it on him. Straddling him, she sank down on his thick cock until he was deep inside her.

"Look at me," he ordered and her entire body quivered.

His big hands steadied her hips.

"You are so fucking beautiful."

Emily moved slowly at first, loving the way he stretched and filled her. Deep and wide, he felt incredible.

"I want to fuck you all night long," he growled.

His words made her wetter and she leaned over to steady herself on his shoulders. Donovan thrust up and he captured her nipple in his mouth. Sucking on it, he undulated his hips and almost slipped out.

"No," she cried out raggedly and bounced hard on him

so he was firmly inside her. The friction and heat were building up into a delicious tension. His fingers tweaked her nipples as their mouths dueled. She had pictured this for so long, wanting to fight with him and then fall into bed and fuck him.

Rolling quickly, Donovan was suddenly on top of her and taking control of the pace. She'd said she wanted it fast and he was providing her with hard, thrilling plunges that made her toes curl.

She wanted his mouth back so she could scream into it. Her body twitched and rose to greet every pump of his hips. Emily dug her nails into his shoulders as the hot rush of her orgasm shook her from head to toe.

"More," she cried out, and he rocked them faster.

She came again as he pinned her legs up over her head and plunged into her, hard and deep. His eyes were intense and the grin he gave her was feral as he lost control. Donovan bit back a few curses and shuddered against her. Releasing her legs, he rocked against her slowly and kissed her again.

"I'm so sorry," he said, licking down her chest, to her belly button. "I have to get back to the group. They're paying me a lot of money and I can't be a bad host."

"I understand," Emily said. "I just wanted to finish what we started before." She caressed his head and tilted her hips up at him.

"We're not finished," he said. "This is to be continued." Then Donovan rolled off her to get dressed.

Feeling smug, she got dressed and shared another lingering kiss with him. "You don't have to walk me out."

"Yeah, I damn well do."

Emily saw a few stragglers on the porch, but based on the noise from downstairs, most of the crew were watching the game. Donovan helped her back on Sunflower and walked with her to the lighted path.

"You shouldn't run into any problems, but if for some reason a hog is around, ride like hell to the barn. Janice's dogs should raise holy hell and scare them off."

"You worry too much."

"And you haven't seen the aggressive hogs I have. Stay safe, sweetheart. I'll see you after the weekend is over and we can spend more quality time together." He ran his hand over her thigh and it was hard to ride away from him.

"Think about me?" she called over her shoulder.

"Bet on it."

Chapter Six

EMILY HAD A rough weekend. Nate was trying to get her to quit before she started, and while she understood that he wanted to give her an idea of the worst-case scenario, he had no idea that she had faced more dire situations with crappier equipment in Ethiopia.

Yesterday, she had helped cut a few sick cows away from the herd and bring them back to the ranch for their veterinarian, Pete Dickerson, to take a look at. She called in a mechanic to fix the Gator and the haying tractor because, of course, both machines decided not to work at the same time.

The icing on the cake, though, was when her father's truck got stuck in the mud and he made her get behind it with the rest of the hands to push it out. If he thought a little mud was going to deter her, he was mistaken.

She hadn't had time to visit Donovan again, though he was probably camping out with his tour group. Emily was barely able to climb the stairs to her bedroom every night. She wouldn't be able to keep up with him in bed tonight anyway.

Monday, however, her father took pity on her and told her to shadow her mother and help her with the accounting and the bills. That was more Janice's area of expertise, but her mother served tea and cookies and not once did Emily step in horse or cow shit.

They were in worse shape financially than she had thought, though. "I figured it was getting better," she said to her mother.

"This is better. I've been able to pay off the back bills, but trying to keep up with the new ones has been a challenge. The rent money helps, of course, but Trent's students pay him and Janice's retreat attendees will also pay her. We need to bring in more money. We can do that by selling some cows off-season, but we won't get a good price." Her mother tapped a date on the calendar. "We're going to sell off a hundred head."

"I've got a few ideas that might help." Once they paid what they could, she helped her mother in the kitchen to prepare supper and then went out front to make a phone call. Now that she had the money, or would once Trent transferred it into her account, she called the number her friend Bobby from the Peace Corps had given her to schedule a meeting about installing the wind turbines.

"Who's this?"

Emily was a little taken aback by the roughness. "Hi, my name is Emily Sullivan. Bobby Reeves gave me your number. I'm looking for Jules St. John?"

"This is he." The voice smoothed out into a more professional tone.

"I want to get some wind turbines placed on my land and he said you could help me with that."

"Have you had the land tested?"

"Tested for what?"

"If there are enough wind currents to power a turbine."

"Oh. No, I haven't."

"How many were you looking to put up?"

At forty thousand each, she could only afford six. Emily nibbled on her lip. But that wouldn't leave her with much left over from Trent's loans. She decided to play it safe, even though it was killing her not to wring all the profit she could from it. The ranch would still have bills to pay and saving some of the loan money gave them a cushion that could set her parents' minds at ease.

"Five," she said before she could change her mind.

"Five?"

"That's all I can afford right now," she said defensively.

"You should have at least double that to start off."

"Well, unless you can give me ten wind turbines for the cost of five, it will have to do for now."

There was a long pause and then the man said, "Do you have enough land available for ten wind turbines?"

"I have enough for fifteen." She snorted. What did it matter? She only had the money for five.

"We could rent you ten and you could pay them off through installments."

"You're kidding?" Emily's back straightened and she gazed off into the distance while desperately trying to do the math in her head. "That would be perfect. How fast could you get them in?" The faster they were in, the sooner she could start repaying the loan and the rental fees. Fifteen could bring in almost $120,000 in one year.

"Well, first I need to do a test of the lands. That's going to run you five thousand dollars."

Emily winced. That was half her savings.

"However, if the land proves viable for the turbines, that test fee will apply as a credit on your account."

That didn't sound so bad. "How much will this cost me total?"

"I'll need another five thousand dollars to set you up in our system and get the equipment in place. From there, we'll take half of the output for the next five years."

"That sounds good." It would delay her paying Trent back, but once she was free and clear, the ranch wouldn't have to worry about being profitable ever again.

"At the end of five years, we'll offer to sell you the wind turbines at a substantial discount."

She was beginning to get excited. "This all sounds great. When can we get started?"

"As soon as you wire me the first five-thousand-dollar payment."

"I can do that today," Emily said, eager to pay off some of the ranch bills before they became overdue. "How soon can you come out and do your test?" It was a risk. If the land wasn't viable, she was out five thousand dollars. But she had to try. This renewable energy would not only help the environment, but also keep her family's electricity bill low. It had to work. It just had to. And if these sixty acres didn't work, they could try another sixty.

"Let me get some information, then, and I'll tell you

where to wire the money."

"I'll go get a pen." Emily hurried inside and climbed the stairs to her room. She took down the information and gave him the address of the ranch. "Can you come out this week?"

"When I receive confirmation of the wire, I'll set up a time to conduct the tests. It will probably be this week. We'll definitely be in touch."

"Great." Emily got off the phone feeling confident and in charge. She'd had the weekend from hell doing physical work and this morning was proving to be challenging mentally, but she was coping. She would make her parents believe in her yet. Emily was looking forward to the day when she could relinquish the title of baby to Alissa.

AS SOON AS the last hunter left that morning, Donovan cleaned up after them and then took a shower. He'd seen some signs of a group of elk moving through the areas they had been hunting in, so he had set up a hunting blind this weekend. They didn't see any elk, but Donovan was sure they were visiting the pond to drink and graze. However, he didn't want to risk the white elk being seen by the hunting group. Donovan had promised that he would find her and leave her unharmed. He hadn't put that in his hunting contracts because he was still ninety percent sure the ranch hands were playing a joke on him. But just in case they weren't, after setting up a few blinds, he moved his group back toward the easier game.

They brought down a whitetail and a couple of turkeys each, and several hogs. Those damned hogs wouldn't quit. They were getting bold and instead of hiding from humans, they were aggressive. The hunters were pleased. They booked again for next month and he was confident that he could get them elk this time, even though the rutting season would be over by then. He was eager to get back out there this morning on foot to see if he could track the elk and spot the white elk that Nate kept swearing was out there.

If on the off chance he found her, he'd have to mark the trails and bring Kelly back so she could take her photos. Trent wasn't going to be up for all the hiking and strenuous activities, though, so Donovan would ask Nate and a couple of hands to go with them in case they ran into any hogs. The bastards had charged them this weekend and were getting bolder and meaner, the deeper he took the hunters.

He couldn't risk taking the truck or the Gator as deep as he wanted to go. He was hoping the land wasn't too muddy for horses. He was saddling up one of the spare trail horses when Emily caught up with him.

"Hello, darlin'," he said, sweeping her up for a kiss. He was looking forward to having her in his bed all week long, if she wanted to be there. By the enthusiastic way she returned his kiss, he was confident she'd be all right with that. In fact, he wouldn't mind fooling around in the hay before he went.

"Did your tour group have a good time?" she asked when they came up for breath.

He ran his thumb over her lip that was slightly puffy from his kisses. "They're coming back next month."

"Rats," she said.

"Can't win them all." Donovan was reluctant to let her go. "Did you come all this way to see me?"

"Yup, my mother wants me out of her hair and Dad told me to make myself useful, so here I am."

"Useful?"

"He wants me to make your job easier." She rubbed his arm and gave him a saucy look.

"That must chafe your ass something fierce."

"It's ironic, I'll admit it. So where are you off to?"

"I'm going to track this elusive white elk of yours."

She made a face. "Who told you about Ghost?"

"It's an undead elk?"

"No, that's what my sisters call her."

"Wait." He turned to stare at her. "This isn't a joke? You've seen her?"

"We've seen a couple of them. Once when we were kids. Then again about ten years ago. It's not the same one, obviously. They don't live that long. But we've got white ones. Always have." She shrugged.

"Do you know how rare that is?"

"Too rare to be a trophy." She lifted her chin defiantly at him.

"Of course." He stroked her cheek. She was so soft and delicate, she made him feel like a big oaf.

"What do you mean, of course?" She gestured to his rifle bag, which was secured on the back of his horse. "What's that for, then?"

"Hogs." That shut her up.

Emily crossed her arms and looked away.

"I'm hunting for resource management. Not for eradication—except for the feral hogs. They breed too fast to kill off entirely."

"So you're not going to kill Ghost?" Emily eyeballed him disbelievingly.

"No."

"What if your hunters want to hunt her?"

"No."

"What if they pay a lot of money?"

"Still no."

Donovan had to stagger back when she launched herself at him. He was not only getting used to kissing her, it was addicting. He was thinking of putting his horse back into the barn and taking Emily back to the hunting lodge. But just as he started unbuttoning her jeans, she broke away from him.

"Let's go find her."

Chapter Seven

EMILY MISSED TRAIL riding, even though Donovan was taking them through heavy brush. Sunflower was going to be a mess of burrs and mud when they got back. But it was a beautiful November afternoon and she was enjoying the sun and the seventy-degree weather, which reminded her of Ethiopia. The sights, however, couldn't be any more different with the lush carpet of forest and the nearby pond.

"What time are your parents expecting you back?" he asked.

"They're not. Mom roped Dad into going to the tree lighting committee meeting. December is coming up fast."

"They need a committee for that?"

"In Last Stand, there's a committee for everything."

"So you can stay the night with me?"

"I'm not sure I'm ready to flaunt our relationship yet," she said. "My dad's pretty traditional. I don't think he'd stand for a friends with benefits situation."

"Is that what we are?" Donovan asked.

"I'm not sure we're friends."

He barked out a laugh. After a few moments of comfortable silence he said, "I wouldn't mind a girlfriend."

"I'm not sure I want to define us like that."

"Why not?"

"It would have an expiration date on it, wouldn't it? Three years and you're gone."

He disappointed her when he nodded. "That's true."

It was good to get that out in front now, so there wouldn't be any hurt feelings. However, she wasn't really wired for casual relationships. She'd had one boyfriend all through high school. One boyfriend all through college. And she'd had a budding relationship with one of the men working with her in the village in West Tigray. She still kept in contact with all her exes. Maybe she could do that with Donovan. At least until the next boy came along. Except Donovan wasn't a boy. He was a very sexy man and she was afraid she might not get over him quickly if they got involved. She had to protect her heart. He was all wrong for her anyway, but that didn't mean they couldn't have a good time while it lasted.

Sex with Donovan was fun, like zip-lining and off-roading.

"That doesn't mean I don't want to fool around," she said.

"I was worried there for a moment." Donovan grinned.

"As long as we keep it casual." Casual sounded safe. It sounded like something mature adults could agree on. It was a boundary for not getting hurt.

"I don't share, though."

"What's that supposed to mean?" she asked.

"If you're with me, then you're with me. I won't be

sleeping with anyone but you, and you damn well won't be screwing around with anyone else either."

Her lips twitched. "That sounds like you're staking a claim, cowboy."

"Maybe I am."

"I'll think about it."

He whirled to look at her and she blew him a kiss. Closing his eyes, he muttered, "This is a mistake."

"It'll be a fun mistake," she agreed.

They heard the snorting and bugling of elks up ahead. "Let's see how close we can get," he said, urging his horse forward. They clomped through the brush and mud, but it was clear that there wasn't a way they could go much farther. "Let's tie off back there and go forward on foot."

"Is it going to be safe for them?" Ever since the hog episode, Sunflower was a little squirrelly in the woods. But if Donovan's horse was with her, she would take her cues from him.

Donovan unpacked the rifle and extra ammunition. "I've got it covered."

She grimaced and helped secure the horses to trees in a small clearing. "You're not going to shoot an elk today, are you?"

"Not unless you think our horses can carry six hundred pounds back to the ranch house."

"I'm going to barf if you don't knock it off." She stayed behind Donovan as he cleared the way for them. He moved quickly and silently for a big man. Once they pushed through a few overgrown areas, they were in a clearing with a large pond. She heard a barking sound and Donovan motioned her to be quiet. Mewling sounds and another bugle confirmed that there were both cows and bulls up ahead.

He led them toward a tree and she recognized the makeshift steps he had hammered into the trunk.

"Up," he said in a low voice and encouraged her to climb with a friendly hand on her ass. Oh, was that how he wanted to play? This tree stand was sturdy, but didn't have any of the same amenities as the other one. Donovan followed quickly up after her and set his rifle down where it was in easy reach. He immediately began to open the back of the trail camera that had been pointing down toward the pond. He slipped the chip into a reader and sat with his back to the tree.

Cuddling up to him, she peered into the viewer. Donovan wrapped his arm around her and together they watched as he fast-forwarded through the last forty-eight hours. "Bingo," he said, his voice low and intimate.

On screen she saw the elks gathering around the pond, but it was impossible to tell if one of them was their ghost or not. There were different shades of darkness of all the bulls and cows. One was paler than the others and her lack of antlers showed her to be a cow.

"It could be her," she said, feeling excitement tickling her stomach. It would be good to see a white elk again. She and her sisters had always thought seeing one was good luck. The Three Sisters Ranch could use some good luck right about now. Emily looked down at the pond, but there wasn't any activity there.

"Want to wait?" he asked.

"Won't our scent scare them off?"

"Not this far up."

"Do we have to be silent?"

"If we're not disruptive, we could have a conversation. What do you want to talk about, sweetheart?"

"Who says I want to talk?" She grinned at him and pressed her mouth against his.

Kissing him was a lot more fun than fighting with him, that was for sure.

"I'm assuming this means you're done thinking about it?" he said after a long, sensual kiss that curled her toes.

She rested her cheek on his shoulder. "Do you want to sign another three-year lease—this time with me?"

"Only if it's exclusive."

"I can be exclusive. Are you sure you want to risk falling in love with me and having to stay in one place for the rest of your life?"

"Sounds like paradise," he said.

Emily thought he was being a sarcastic jerk, but there was a wistful tone in his voice that made her look up at him, and in that moment, she saw truth and vulnerability in his gray eyes.

"What's stopping you?"

He tried to distract her with a mind-melting kiss and with one of his hands on her breast and the other one on her ass, she had to admit it was working. But then a loud bark, almost underneath them, jolted them apart. While they had been kissing, the herd had sauntered into their area. Looking around, they saw shades of brown and copper. The noisy bull rubbed against their tree and one of the stairs popped off.

"Cock blocker," Donovan muttered.

"I don't see her," Emily said, disappointed.

"Tell me the truth," he said. "Does she really exist or are all of you playing a joke on the new guy?"

"I'll tell you the truth if you tell me one of your secrets."

He tensed. "Who says I have secrets?"

"You're practically the archetype of the mysterious stranger."

Donovan went in to kiss her again, but she stopped him with a reluctant hand on his chest. "Are you in, or are you going to chicken out?"

"All right, you want to play twenty questions instead of making out, let's have at it. Is the ghost elk real?"

"I was telling you the truth before. I've seen a snow-white elk twice in my life."

"Where?"

Emily thought hard. It had been so long ago. "It was on a pasture land. I don't remember which one. Nate might remember."

"He doesn't. Or he doesn't want me to get close to the pasture lands."

"No, he'd tell you. He trusts you."

"Why?" Donovan scoffed.

"Why wouldn't he? And that's a question I want to know, so don't be flip about the answer."

"Sneaky," he said, and rubbed her arm. "I don't come

from good people. Can I leave it at that?"

"You owe me two more questions, so I'm going to ask you to elaborate on it. What do you mean by that?"

Donovan looked like he'd swallowed a lemon. "Can I kiss you again before I answer?"

"You're not going to distract me for long." Emily climbed into his lap and took his face in her hands. She kissed him as if they were the last two people in the world, as if she was trying desperately not to fall in love with him.

Groaning, he held her tight as they rubbed their bodies together. God, she wanted him. Thirty feet in the air, she forgot all about the bugling and snorting elks and concentrated on how his body felt under her. Emily rocked against him, loving the hard feel of him between her thighs.

"I'm going to get off if we don't stop," she whispered against his mouth.

"Why the fuck would we stop?" He claimed her mouth again, his hands busy under her shirt. This time, she was wearing a bra because not wearing one on horseback hurt like a bitch.

Emily used his body to come, arching against him while his mouth branded her with hot, passionate kisses. Her head thrown back, she rode out the sensations clutching his shoulders desperately. "Don't let me fall." She laughed shakily, suddenly too dizzy to move.

"Never." He tucked her in close.

After a moment to come down from the delicious endorphins still spinning wildly through her, she unbuttoned his pants and slid his zipper down.

"What are you doing?" he asked, his breath catching as she leaned over and pulled his cock out of his underwear.

"Figure it out." Emily licked the head of it tasting salt and warm man. "Mmm," she moaned and took him in her mouth.

"Fuck," Donovan ground out, tensing and thrusting his hips up.

She took him deeper and held on to the shaft of his cock while she slowly slid her mouth up and down his length. He wrapped her ponytail around his fist and tugged slightly. Emily liked that and went faster.

"God," he sighed. "Don't stop. Please don't stop."

She didn't plan on it, not when he reacted like this. He was stiff and shaking, his breathing irregular. Swirling her tongue around the tip, Emily teased him. He pulled back on her hair until she looked up at him. His gray eyes had darkened with passion.

"Take off your pants," he growled.

"No." She went back to sucking on him. With her luck, they'd kick her jeans off the tree stand and she'd be bare-assed in the middle of nowhere. They could save the love-making until they got back. Right now, she was enjoying herself too much to stop.

"Emily," he choked out.

"Mmm." She liked when he called out her name.

"Emily," he said louder.

Oh yeah, scream it, baby. She went faster and sucked harder.

Donovan groaned long and loud. His fingers loosened in

her hair and he came in short, jerky bursts. Swallowing and then licking him once last time, she rose up to kiss him.

"I saw her," he said.

"What?" She whipped her head to the pond and then looked around.

Donovan chuckled as he fixed himself up. "She wandered through, east to west." He pointed.

"Are you shitting me?" she hissed. "I missed her."

"I tried to tell you."

"You didn't try that hard," she said tartly.

He kissed her hard on the mouth. "No, I didn't. I was enjoying myself too much. Holy hell, where did you learn how to drive a man crazy like that?"

"Girl Scouts."

Donovan choked on a laugh. "What?"

"Actually, it was my crazy summer with that biker gang. Is that better? Jesus, Donovan, what kind of question is that?"

"Give me a break, you blew my mind. I don't have a lot of gray matter left."

"Apparently." She frowned at him, but couldn't be mad at him. He really looked dazed. "Did you really see her?"

"Clear as day. You were amazing, but she's pure white and caught my eye."

"I can't believe I missed her."

"We'll stay awhile longer. She might saunter through again. Come here, darlin'. I want you in my arms."

That sounded good to her and she cuddled next to him, hugging him tight. "You're not off the hook, you know."

He sighed deep. "I figured."

"I'm waiting for you to explain what you meant about your family not being good people."

Playing with her hair, Donovan said, "Do you know what a grifter is?"

"A con man?"

"My father was their king. He should have been a movie star. He could take on any role and make you believe anything. He could convince you he was a beggar with a heart of gold who just needed one more chance to live his best life. Or he could be old money looking to invest his fortune in a scheme, only he needed your money as well to make you both rich beyond your wildest dreams. He stole from a lot of people. He hurt a lot of people. He had his hand in everything from drugs to espionage. He's a piece of work."

Emily rubbed her cheek on his arm. "You're not your father."

"I never was that talented or I might have been. My mother was from the streets. She could pick your pocket while you were wearing the tightest jeans or steal the rings from your fingers when she shook your hand. She could have been a magician. She enchanted you from the moment you laid eyes on her. They met when Charlie caught her taking his wallet. Instead of breaking her fingers, he married her. They had me."

Donovan dangled her keys in front of her face. She slapped her front pocket and of course they were gone. She hadn't felt him move. Hadn't heard the keys jingle. "That's a cool party trick."

"It's makes working the rodeo a lot more interesting. That's how I grew up. We moved from town to town, changing cars and locations when things got too hot. I never went to school. We were never in one place for very long. But by the time I was ten, I could play a mark like a fiddle. Who needed schools or jobs when the money was right there for the taking? Then one day, we had a house in Colleyville. I was enrolled in high school. I was fourteen and had never attended a day of school in my life. But I was a good actor with fake transcripts so I played my part well."

"What was your part?"

"I was to befriend the son of a prominent computer engineer. Samuel Barton was a geeky kid, so it was easy. Too easy. We hung out at each other's houses. We got really close. On sleepovers, I would memorize their floor plan. I knew where the safe was, where his mother hid her jewelry, and where she kept the roll of bills she hid from her husband. But we weren't after money or fencible items. I didn't know what the plan was. My father didn't tell me. Weeks turned into months and I entered my sophomore year of high school. My folks and I played our parts so well, I started to believe I was Jared King and my father was a financial planner."

Donovan went so still and quiet, Emily raised her head just to make sure Ghost hadn't come back into view.

"What happened?"

He let out a shuddering breath. "He fleeced the wrong man. The cryptocurrency scheme he was running was starting to collapse and instead of cutting and running, my dad got greedy. He brought my mother and me over to the Bartons' place to appeal to Samuel's dad that all he needed was more time. That everything was on the up and up." Donovan shook his head. "Even though the mark was a computer engineer, he figured out the scam. He had been expecting my father to come alone."

Emily gripped him tightly. She didn't want to hear the end of the story, but Donovan continued to speak in an emotionless, flat voice, and she knew that he was far away. He was back in that rich neighborhood in Colleyville.

"He wanted his money back. When my father tried to spin the situation, the mark pulled a gun. They started screaming at each other. My mother grabbed my arm and tried to leave, but there were men, bodyguards, blocking the door. We backed up. It happened so fast then. Samuel flew down the stairs yelling for his dad to stop. My father shoved me at the mark and tried to run past him. My mother lunged for me. The gun went off. When it was all over, my mother was shot. She took a bullet meant for me while my father escaped out the back door."

"Holy shit, Donovan." Emily climbed into his lap and pressed her face against his. She would do anything to bring him back to her, but he was still in that far-off place.

"Before she bled out on the carpet, she convinced the mark that she had no idea what was going on. That we were innocent and she didn't understand why the mark shot her. She was so convincing, one of the bodyguards who had blocked us from leaving started to cry. She died before the ambulance came. I thought it was a brilliant con. Her best yet. Even I couldn't find her pulse. I couldn't wait until we could talk about how she did it. So I acted my best, wailing and crying, trying to sell her performance. It wasn't until her funeral, when I saw her in the open casket, that I truly believed it was real." He laughed shakily, tears flowing down his cheeks. "I had asked the funeral director to give us a few minutes alone." He wiped his face with his sleeve. "I leaned into the casket and asked her what our next move was. 'Come on, Mom, we're alone. Okay fine, don't break character. Twitch a finger—you're freaking me out.' And then I touched her." Donovan shuddered.

"I'm so sorry," she whispered.

"It was a long time ago," he said. "Fuck, I've never told anyone this."

"What happened after that?"

"I could have walked away scot-free. My mother had died protecting me in more ways than one."

"You didn't do anything wrong."

He shrugged. "That's debatable. But I couldn't just walk away from what happened. I knew how it would go if I did. I would go to the library in the next town and wait for him to show up, like we had arranged if anything ever went bad. That was the way we would find each other again. Then he'd spin me a line of bullshit and we would lay low for a while until he found another mark. If my mother hadn't died, I probably would have done just that. It was the only life I knew."

"But your father put you in the line of fire to save his

own ass."

Donovan nodded. "I was the expendable one. I wasn't as talented as my mother or as smart as my father."

"That's bullshit." Emily tried to keep her voice down, so she wouldn't startle the elk, but she couldn't help it. "You were his son."

"I think 'father' was just another role he played. I couldn't let him go unpunished for my mother's death. I lawyered up and traded information for immunity. My father was eventually caught after I gave the cops every alias I could think of and showed them where they could find secret stashes all over Texas. I testified against him at his trial, emancipated myself, and changed my last name to Link. They threw the book at him. My father has been in prison ever since." Kissing her on the top of her head, he said shakily, "So that's what I meant when I said I don't come from good people. I bet you're sorry you asked."

"Not even close."

They hung around for a few more hours, but the white elk never came back in sight. Donovan didn't say anything more. Emily had been content to hold on to him and he was so quiet, a few times she had to check and see if he had fallen asleep. Each time, though, he was staring off into space with a thousand-yard stare.

When it was time to head back to the ranch, Emily was desperate to reach him. Sunflower was eager to get back to the barn, so the ride wasn't a good time to talk. But as they were putting the horses in their stalls, Emily couldn't stand the silence any longer.

"Do you want some company tonight?"

"I think I need some space. I hadn't expected to unload my torrid past on you like that." He gave her a rueful smile.

"I'm glad you trusted me enough to tell me. If it means anything, I trust you, too. And I think your past doesn't need to color your future. I know you're a good man, an honest one. You don't have to keep running from your past."

He finished brushing his horse and gave him feed and water. "I used to think you were right. But I got a letter from my father—from prison—the other day. He knows where I am and what I'm doing. I don't know how. He always seems to track me if I stay in one place for long. One of these days he's going to con his way into getting parole and he's going to show up here. He's bad news and I don't want to ever see him again. And I certainly don't want you or your family to be involved with him. He can't be trusted."

"So that's why you're not going to stay?"

"That's why, sweetheart. It's got nothing to do with you." He rubbed her shoulder. "The Lincoln men are nothing but trouble."

"Well, then it's a good thing you're not a Lincoln, Donovan Link." She hugged him and after a moment, his arms went around her and he hugged her back.

Chapter Eight

EMILY WAITED AT the end of the driveway for Jules St. John to arrive. She needed to show him the sixty acres of land where she wanted to build the wind turbines so he could perform the very expensive test she'd paid for. She didn't want to tell her family until after the tests results were back, but she was certain the area was perfect for wind energy. She had done some research online.

She had been hoping that Donovan would go out riding with them, but he hadn't returned her call yet. He'd been a little distant and subdued ever since he told her about his parents. She guessed he was probably regretting it because she hadn't seen him around these past few days. Of course, he was out tracking elk during the day and at night, and since she wasn't sure he wanted company, she was giving him his space.

Donovan had set up the field camera so he could monitor it remotely and track the elks' progress. Once he had a good idea where they went on their migration, he had said he would clear a path and set up a place for Kelly to take her pictures in safety.

It was strange that after so many months of resenting

him, Emily was beginning to get used to him. She wondered if she haunted his thoughts the way he did hers. She wished she knew what to say to him that would make things better. Emily considered opening up to him too about her feelings of never being good enough for her father, but it didn't seem such a big deal compared to his experiences. Her father was an angry and difficult man, but he'd never throw her or her sisters in front of a gunman.

Emily was just about to give up on Jules when a shiny new Toyota Camry pulled into the ranch. Flagging him down, she got into the passenger's seat. "Hi, I'm Emily." She held out her hand to him.

"It's nice to meet you. I'm Jules." He shook her hand. He was a silver-haired older man with a friendly open face. Laugh lines creased around his eyes and mouth. Jules was dressed in a crisp button-down shirt and brand-new blue jeans. She hoped he didn't mind getting a little dirty because the land they were going to ride over was muddy and overrun.

"Just drive straight and park at the farmhouse. We're going to have to ride out to the land. Do you have a lot of equipment?"

"Just my barometer and my laptop."

"Oh." Emily didn't know why the testing cost so much if that was all he was going to use. But he had said that if the land was approved, she could use the testing fee as credit to rent the wind turbines.

It had to be approved. She was running out of ideas.

There was still no sign of Donovan, so Emily saddled up

Sunflower and Kelly's horse, Pippi, for Jules. He rode stiffly, like he wasn't used to the saddle. She didn't want to ask her father to borrow the truck because he would have wanted to know why. And she didn't trust the ATVs not to break down. They had been giving them trouble lately and she wanted to impress Jules so he didn't think they were desperate for the money the wind turbines would bring in.

Even if they were.

"So how do you know Bobby Reeves?" she asked once they were on the trails heading out.

"Who?"

"He's the one who gave me your number."

"Oh right, Robert."

Emily smiled. No one called Bobby "Robert." He hated it. It sounded too stiff.

"I went to school with his brother-in-law, John. We see each other socially when he's back in town. I haven't seen him in a while."

"That's because he's doing back-to-back contracts in the Peace Corps."

Jules nodded. "I thought I heard that he was volunteering. Is that where you know him from?"

"Yes, we worked together in West Tigray for a while."

"How long have you been back?"

"A few months. My parents needed some help around the farm and I'm trying to make things profitable for them as they get older."

"That's smart. How much land do you have?"

"Five thousand acres."

"I bet your cattle love all that room."

"They're a handful, but we manage to build up our herds each year so we can sell a bunch at market."

Jules smiled. "It sounds very Old West. I've just moved here recently so this is all new to me. I've been working in California mostly. I've recently expanded my business here."

They rode out for about an hour before they reached the acres her father had given her. She was surprised and pleased to see Donovan in the distance. She flagged him down by waving wildly until he saw them. His horse picked his way through the scrub brushes and overgrowth.

"Who's that?" Jules frowned.

"My boyfriend," Emily said, trying the label out for the first time. If Donovan wanted an exclusive relationship for three years, she decided he would be her boyfriend. She dismounted and gave him a hug and a kiss. "I missed you," she said. "Why didn't you call? We would have waited for you or met up with you sooner."

"No signal out here," Donovan said, glancing at Jules as he set up his equipment.

"Yes, I see that." Jules tapped a few things on his computer.

"Is that going to be a problem?" she asked.

"It will delay my results, but I'll send them to you as soon as I compile the data and have internet."

"Sounds good."

Donovan leaned against a tree with his arms crossed as Jules set up his barometer and took readings in several places. Jules jotted down notes in a small notebook.

"Any luck on the white elk?" she asked.

Donovan shook his head. He looked tired and frustrated. "I know what I saw."

"I believe you. Remember, I've seen her before. Or her mother and grandmother." She rubbed his arm. "I think you're working too hard."

"I promised the next hunting group that we'd go after elk."

Emily stiffened. "What?"

"So I need to make sure that we don't go anywhere near where the white elk might be. Don't worry. If I can nail it down, I'll make them sign agreements that the white elk are off-limits."

"Do you honestly think that will work? Are you going to make them pinkie promise, too?" Emily crossed her arms over her chest, but Donovan wasn't looking at her. He was staring at Jules, who was picking his way through the scrub brushes.

"What did you say you needed this moron for?"

"Donovan, shh. Don't say stuff like that. He's testing the acres to see if there's enough wind going through here to power the turbines."

"Watch out for the rattlers," Donovan called out.

Jules flinched and jumped. "Rattlers?"

"How much is this costing you?" Donovan asked her in a lowered voice.

"Five thousand."

"Five thousand?" Donovan cried.

Emily tried to hush him.

"You're being hustled."

"No, I'm not. He came highly recommended."

Jules came hurrying back to them. "Is this the entire property?"

"It's all we have allotted for the wind farm," Emily said.

"I see." Jules sighed. "I'm not sure the wind speed is where we need it to be, but I'll have to get my lab to do some more testing."

"Keep in mind that we'll clear the area, too. I'm not sure if that affects the aerodynamics of your testing," Emily said.

"How can the air currents on the ground be accurate?" Donovan asked. "Shouldn't you at least climb a tree and find out what they are from up there?"

Jules smiled condescendingly at Donovan. "Of course, that's one way to do it. Before computer technology assisted us, the surveyors would build a costly tower to take the readings from. Now we use a computer algorithm to extrapolate the raw data I take in the field."

"Uh-huh," Donovan drawled, unconvinced.

"I think you'll find it's very windy here," Emily broke in, looking from one to the other.

"But is it the windiest place on your ranch?" Jules asked. "The more wind power you have, the more money you'll make."

"I'm not sure," Emily said, biting her lip. Would her father be willing to give her more land if this didn't work out? Or would he think she was beating a dead horse about this "wind turbine nonsense"?

"This plot of land is indicative of the rest of the ranch,"

Donovan said. "You don't need to see any other part of it. In fact, I think you should leave."

"Donovan," Emily gasped. He was always brusque and gruff, but this was damned rude.

"No, your boyfriend is right. I've gotten all I need here. Now it's up to the computer to let us know if we can start building or not."

As they made their way back to the horses, Jules was staring at the ground intently. He nearly vaulted into the saddle.

"Should I have a crew come out and clear the place to prepare?" Emily asked. "I mean maybe if you don't get good enough readings, we could try putting up a tower for better readings, like Donovan suggested."

She was starting to get worried. What if Donovan was right and Jules was trying to scam her? She only had Bobby's word that this guy was on the up and up.

"So what other projects have you worked on around here?" she asked.

"To tell you the truth, there hasn't been a lot in the Medina Valley. We had one former vineyard turn unproductive acres into a profitable wind farm, but we had our doubts at first." Jules shrugged. "Sometimes the wind power just isn't there. That's why we test. No sense in laying out all that money if you're not going to see a decent profit."

Emily nodded. There had to be a way to do better on these wind tests. She could hire Sykes construction to come back here with their backhoes and get them ready for the turbines. She had gone to school with Chris Sykes and they'd offered to put her sisters on a payment plan when they hired them to clear land for Janice's retreat center. Maybe she could convince Jules to install a wind turbine anyway and they could get real-time results. Emily was not ready to give up. Not when she was so close to getting a new revenue stream in for the ranch.

"I'm positive our software will be accurate." Jules oozed self-assurance, but Emily didn't know whether to be confident or worried.

"I bet you are," Donovan muttered, and very deliberately took his rifle out of the canvas bag he had attached to the back of his saddle.

"Donovan?" Emily asked. She glanced around, wondering if there were hogs in the area. Straining her ears, she didn't hear anything.

He sighted the rifle and Jules flinched back, even though it wasn't pointed anywhere near him.

Pippi danced away at the hard pull on her reins. Emily winced. "Don't do that," she said to Jules. "She has a soft mouth."

After a second, Donovan lowered the rifle and continued riding.

"What was that all about?" Jules said, his voice high-pitched.

"I thought I saw a snake."

"Why didn't you shoot it?"

Donovan flicked a glance at her. "It slithered away. Be careful out here. They like to hide in plain sight and when you least expect it, they'll rear up and strike."

Emily didn't know exactly where he was going with this.

He had pointed the rifle at a tree and not on the ground. Since she wasn't planning on climbing a tree that didn't have a stand in it, she had a feeling he was trying to scare Jules.

"Knock it off," she muttered to him.

"We need to talk."

"I've been trying to talk to you all week. And don't think you're off the hook for the elk hunting. I don't trust the hunters not to conveniently forget they're not supposed to trophy hunt a rare elk."

"These men are looking for sport, not trophies. They're using the meat, not only for themselves but they're also donating it to food kitchens in the city."

"Yeah, they're real saints."

"But at least they're not rooking me out of my hard-earned money, like this asshole."

"Donovan, he can hear you."

"I know he can. And trust me, he and I are going to have words." Donovan looked at Jules fiercely.

"Emily, I don't want to cause any problems. It seems like you're not ready to bring in the wind turbines." Jules gave her a small smile and shook his head.

"Yes," Donovan said at the same time she said, "No."

"You have my number. When you're ready to get started, just give me a call."

"No," Emily repeated. "It's my land. Donovan is being overprotective. When you spend your life as a hammer, everything looks like a nail."

Chapter Nine

DONOVAN WAS GOING to show her a hammer all right. When they got back to the barn, he left Emily to deal with taking care of the three horses so he and Jules St. John could have a little talk.

"Donovan, get back here and help me with these guys," Emily said, her hands full with the three horses that needed to be watered, untacked, and groomed.

"I'll be right back." He grabbed Jules by the arm and propelled him out of the barn.

"Donovan," she warned.

"It's all right, Emily. I'm sure he's just concerned. I'll put his mind at ease," Jules said, shaking him off.

"It's not his business to be concerned," Emily grumbled.

"Wrong," Donovan told her.

When they cleared her earshot, Donovan said, "I saw you."

"I don't know what you're talking about." Jules clasped his hands behind his back and rocked on his heels.

"You dropped something back there. What was it? A GPS or a tracker so you and your buddies can find your way back here through the forest land and rob us blind?"

"You, sir, are paranoid."

"You're damn right I am."

"Just what am I supposed to steal back there in snake-infested lands? Dirt?"

Donovan longed to wipe the smirk off his face with a well-timed punch in the jaw. "How about equipment or supplies that disappear from your bogus job site that you'll bill back to Emily?"

Jules's jaw clenched. "I find your accusations insulting."

"Let me guess about these tests. You're not going to find enough wind power, not because it's not there, but because you don't have the right equipment. That's not going to stop you from billing her for another test for another parcel of property."

"I'd be more than happy to take you and Miss Sullivan on a tour of our facilities to show you that we have adequate resources."

"Let's go. Right now."

Jules sighed. "Very well, get in the car."

Donovan had the first ping of doubt. Jules hadn't seemed to be slick enough to have set up a long-term con complete with office equipment and workers who may or may not be in on the con. That was a lot of work for a four-figure paycheck.

"Did my father send you?" Donovan asked. If his father was bankrolling this from prison as a means to get a foot into Donovan's hunting business, Emily's money would just be an added bonus.

"I don't even know your last name, sir." A slight crease in

his brow. Genuine confusion? Then Jules's face settled back into the haughty mask he was hiding behind. "Now, I can understand that you're concerned about your girlfriend, but I assure you..."

"Save it." Donovan was going to go all in. If he was being paranoid and Jules was an honest businessman, it would come out in Jules's reactions. Donovan would be able to read his face. If he was dirty, when Donovan turned up the heat on him that would also show in his body language and attitude. "Let me *assure you*, I know the bank account she wired the five thousand dollars to is shielded and by the time the bank authorizes a reversal of payments, the funds and you will be long gone. Or so you think. You fucked up." Donovan made himself sound contemptuous to try to prick Jules's pride.

"I am an honest businessman and I resent the implications that I am not. I'm leaving." Jules took the high road and kept calm. As he lifted his chin at him, Jules's eyes reflected anger, but not outrage. He didn't try to convince him that he was innocent. He was gaslighting Donovan.

"In the rental car?" Donovan said slowly.

Jules paused with his hand on the driver's-side door. His eyes flicked to the barn and then back to Donovan. Jules plastered on a friendly smile. "I think there has been a misunderstanding."

Gotcha.

"Yeah. There would have been cameras in the rental office. You and I both know the license you used to rent it was false. But the cameras still caught your face. Or the face of your accomplice. And I took a few cell phone shots of you when you weren't looking. Like I said, you got sloppy because you thought you found an easy mark in Emily."

Jules looked over Donovan's shoulder again and set his jaw. Donovan figured it was Emily coming to ream him out. But she needed to hear this first. She needed to see that her trust in Jules was misplaced. Jules had preyed on her innocence, just like his father had done with multiple people. Donovan couldn't change the past, but he could make up for it by shutting this asshole down.

"I have a business relationship with Miss Sullivan and I plan on honoring it, even with your heinous accusations."

"I already know how the scam runs. You're going to pretend your bullshit data is going to give a result that the land doesn't give enough kilowatts or whatever it is to justify a wind farm. She's out five thousand dollars and you close up shop until the next mark comes along. Or—" Donovan said suddenly, "if you thought you could get more money out of her, or if you thought she was going to make a fuss over losing the five thousand dollars, you would tell her that it's her lucky day and you'll need another small investment before you start building. And if you were better at this, you could milk the con another couple of months before cleaning her and maybe her family and friends out as well."

Jules narrowed his eyes at him. "You can't prove any of this. I haven't done any of that. I've done nothing wrong."

"Yet. Put the money back in her account."

"My time is valuable. An agreement was made between myself and Miss Sullivan in good faith."

"You haven't started any work yet. Refund her five thousand dollars."

"That's impossible."

"It's not and you know it. It will be unpopular, especially if you've got partners in this. But I'll tell you what's going to be even more unpopular. Me, getting into your business. If you return her money, leave these people alone, and get out of Texas, I won't burn your operation to the ground."

"Who the fuck do you think you are?" Jules sneered. There it was. The face of a cornered rat. But it was an actual question. Jules didn't know Charlie Lincoln was his father. Donovan didn't know if that was a relief or not.

"Someone who has done it before."

"Good luck, asshole." If Jules could throw someone in Donovan's path to save his own ass, he would have. Instead he leapt into the car fast as a snake.

Donovan lunged for him, and almost got his fingers slammed in the door. Jules started it up and his tires squealed as he pulled away. Donovan jumped back so he didn't get his toes run over and glared after him. Whirling, he found Frank Sullivan approaching him at a fast clip. His face was red and he was visibly shaking.

Shit. This wasn't good. "How much did you hear?" Donovan asked.

"Enough. Are we going after him?"

"Let me handle this."

"Don't coddle me, boy." Frank was breathing hard.

"His type doesn't like being chased down. If he knows what's good for him, he'll return the money."

"We need to call the police, then," Frank gritted out, but he followed Donovan as he headed toward the ranch house and not the barn. Donovan needed to give Emily the heads-up about this.

"He hasn't done anything wrong yet, so the police can't do anything about it yet. If he's smart, he'll return the money and leave. He's been caught and given a chance to disappear. He'd be an idiot not to take it." Donovan shook his head. There was no way Jules was going to return the money. Charlie Lincoln wouldn't have. Donovan hadn't been that much of a threat for Jules to consider passing up on the easy payday. But he would try his damnedest to track him down and make him regret it. Donovan was a hunter and he'd make sure Jules St. John wouldn't run an easy con ever again.

"He didn't strike me as the smart type," Frank said.

Unfortunately, Donovan agreed with him. "The police still can't do anything until he commits a crime. If he cuts and runs, he'll make mistakes. The police can catch him that way." Maybe.

"What about my daughter's money?"

Donovan sighed. "It's already gone."

Frank flinched and went to go toward the barn.

"Wait. Let me talk with Emily, see if I can get some clues. I might be able to find this guy before he takes off. He's left some big trails. If I can track him down, I might be able to get Emily's money back."

Frank thought about it. "You beat it out of him if you have to."

Donovan gave him a tight nod. It wasn't his first plan of action, but he wasn't opposed to it.

Rubbing his hand over his face, Frank suddenly looked tired and defeated. "If I was ten years younger…"

Donovan didn't know what to tell him, but he tried his best. "Men like him don't discriminate. They use people's belief that the world is a good place, then they abuse that trust. Emily isn't at fault here. That's solely on this Jules St. John guy or whatever his real name is."

"Emily should have known better." Frank shook his head and wearily trudged up the porch stairs. "I thought spending time in the Peace Corps would have made her grow up a little, but instead it just fueled her unrealistic ideals."

"She thought she was doing the right thing." Donovan didn't want her father to blame Emily. "This asshole is a crook. It's no different than if he snatched her purse on the street."

"I appreciate what you're doing, Donovan. She needs someone like you to look out for her."

Donovan shook his head in disagreement. "No, she can handle herself. I just happened to be around."

"Well, thank you for being there anyway." Frank went into the house, closing the screen door quietly behind him.

Crap.

Emily was fuming as she took care of the three horses. She had them watered and had removed their tack, but she was busy grooming Sunflower. "What the hell was that all about? And grab a currycomb while you're talking."

Donovan did and headed for the horse he had been riding.

"No, do Pippi first. Otherwise she gets unreasonable."

"She's a horse," Donovan said. "They're always unreasonable."

"Like a lot of men, I know," she said, glaring at him. "I need these wind turbines to get installed and I don't have the money to do it. Jules St. John is my last shot at getting this done quickly. I had a look at our ledgers. We need this. Please tell me you didn't blow it." She threw down the currycomb she was using. "Please."

Donovan saw the desperation in her face and knew that this is what Jules St. John had been preying on.

"Honey, Jules is a con man."

He saw the emotions war for control on her face: disbelief, anger, fear. Snatching up the comb, she went back to her horse. "You don't know that."

Torn between giving her false hope and crushing her with the reality, Donovan avoided the question in her voice. "How did you find out about him?"

"When I was in West Tigray and my father's message came in about coming home to say goodbye to the farm before he sold it, I was floored. I didn't want to lose my home. I went on a mission to save it. I talked to everyone I could about ways to utilize the land to be more profitable. I mean, that's what we were doing in Africa, right? But farming and irrigation were things we were already doing back here and that wasn't helping." Emily continued brushing her horse. "My supervisor suggested the wind turbines, and a friend of mine said that he knew someone who did that sort of thing and I should contact him when I got back to the States."

"What was your friend's name?"

"Bobby Reeves. He's a good man. An honest man. He wouldn't have tried to cheat me."

Donovan had his doubts, but it would give the police a place to start looking for Jules if it came to that. "What was his connection to Jules?"

"A friend of his brother-in-law's," Emily said.

"Walk me through how you contacted Jules and exactly what he said."

As he listened, he took care of Pippi, who was such a sweet horse. He gave her a peppermint at the end of her grooming, which earned him the side-eye from a gorgeous Andalusian in the next stall. Emily's face grew grim when Donovan told her he saw him drop something out in the old pasture.

"Why didn't you tell him he dropped it?" she asked.

"I wanted to come back later and be waiting for whatever he sent."

"Are you sure it's a tracker?"

"I'm going to go look. And bring it back to the lodge."

"Can we use that as evidence?" Emily looked up at him hopefully.

"Sure, but it doesn't point to anything unless he acts on it. Which he won't, because he knows we're onto him."

"Damn it," she whispered, and hugged Sunflower, burying her face in her neck.

"I'm sorry, sweetheart," he said. The only bright side

about any of this was it didn't appear his father wasn't behind it. He had been worried because the timing of his father's letter and the appearance of Jules St. John had been a little too coincidental for him. Still, this was what the Sullivan family had in store if Charlie Lincoln ever got involved with them. He'd have to make sure they knew how to spot a grifter before Donovan's lease was up. That way, he could leave without worrying about them.

Walking over to Emily, he gently took her into his arms. "You're getting Sunflower all wet."

"I'm not crying," she said into his shirt.

He hugged her tighter, anger rippling through him. "I'll get your money back," he said.

"How?"

"Trust me." If he had to, he'd wire it back into her bank account from his own savings. He'd just have to book more tours, that was all. "I told him to give the money back or we'd press charges. If he was telling the truth and he is connected to your friend's brother-in-law, the police may be able to track him down."

"What if he was just pretending to be his friend, like..." Emily cut herself off, but he knew what she was going to say. She stepped out of his arms and went over to the horse he had been riding to groom him.

"Like I did?" Donovan started to organize the tack area and clean up a bit. It gave him something to do with his hands that didn't involve punching the walls.

"I didn't mean it like that."

"I know, but unless Bobby's family is very rich, that isn't

likely."

"I can't believe I screwed this up."

He sighed. He was going to have to make things worse. "Your father heard me confront Jules."

Emily's knees actually wobbled.

"It's okay. I talked him down. He's in the house with your mother."

"Did he get upset? Because his heart isn't that strong."

"He was pissed, but not out of control." Not like the way he was when he had punched out Trent a few months ago.

"Shit," she said. "What can we do? Can we track him down?"

"Let the police handle it. We'll give him a few hours and call him. If the phone's been disconnected, we can bring them into it. If he answers, we can try to get him to meet with us. In the meantime, we can narrow down where he rented the Camry from."

"Do you know how many car dealers there are in Texas?" she groaned.

"Or you can go inside and talk to your father."

"Car dealers it is."

Chapter Ten

AFTER TWO HOURS, the money wasn't back in her account and the phone number she used to contact Jules just kept ringing. She sent an email to Bobby, asking him for his brother-in-law's name and contact information. Hopefully they would get a lead that way. The car rental place was turning out to be a needle in a haystack, but at least she felt like she was doing something.

"Are you ready to call the police?" Donovan asked.

They were in his office. He was at his desk searching car dealerships on his computer and she was on her phone. "Not yet."

When she brought the police into this, it would become real. And if it was real, she was out five thousand dollars that she really couldn't afford to lose.

"Did you do this to a lot of people?"

"Yes." Donovan sighed.

"What a shitty way to earn a living. Why did your father do it?"

"He liked it. He like feeling superior and tricking people. It was a rush for him. Like how some people gamble on the horses, he gambled on people. But just like the track, it's never a sure thing and eventually you lose."

"So you think tricking me gave Jules a rush?"

"If it did, my calling him out soured it for him."

"I suppose that's something," Emily said. "Do you think he feels stupid now? Violated?"

"And afraid he's going to jail. Trust me, he's having a worse night than you."

"Good," she said. "Did your mother feel the same way? Was she addicted to the rush?"

"She liked stealing. She was a magpie. She saw something bright and shiny and she had to have it. It didn't matter if it belonged to someone else or not. If she wanted it, she took it."

"Did you like it?"

"I liked pleasing my parents. I liked their compliments. I hated their disappointments. I never thought about how the marks felt. Not until Samuel Barton became my friend. I guess I thought that when we moved to Colleyville, that was our last con. It wasn't. It was just the longest."

"Did you ever wonder what happened to Samuel and his father?"

"I didn't have to wonder. His father did some time for manslaughter. Ten years and he was out on good behavior." Donovan huffed out a humorless laugh. "He missed his son growing up for taking my mother away from me. Ten years doesn't seem like such a long time for killing someone. My father got thirty for all his scams. Samuel hunted me down a few years ago."

"Why?"

"He was pissed. I disappeared without a trace. He lost his father, his best friend, and his life got turned completely upside down. All because of my father."

"What happened?"

"I let him beat the shit out of me."

"Oh, Donovan."

She came over to him, pushed the chair he was sitting on back from the desk, and straddled his lap. Hugging him tight, she asked, "Why would you do that?"

"Because I deserved it. Don't worry, I had taken worse beatings."

"Is that supposed to make it better?"

"It did for him, at least for a while. Every now and then, though, he tries to contact me again."

"Maybe he wants to apologize?" Emily said.

Donovan stroked her cheek. "More likely, he wants to go another round. But he's been quiet these past few years. Last time I checked, he was living in Silicon Valley and working at a tech firm. His mother divorced his father. I don't know what happened to her, but his father sails around the world on his sailboat."

"I think it's time you stopped blaming yourself for what your father did. He ruined their lives and yours. If anything, you have that in common. Don't let Samuel or anyone in his family beat you up again. It's not your beating to take."

"Sweetheart, I don't plan on ever even seeing him again. Any of them."

"Good. My situation seems so small compared to that. You must think I'm a baby."

"No." He hugged her to him. "I have lots of thoughts about you, but I think you're all woman. And you're all mine."

For the time being. She smiled sadly at him. Unless she could get him to stay. The more time she spent with him, the more she got used to their arguments. She became aware that they were in a rather fun position and hopped up on his desk.

"Why don't you come here and show me that I'm all yours." Emily crooked her finger at him.

"Now, why would I fuck you on my desk when there is a perfectly good bed right in here?" Donovan scooped her up and she wrapped her legs around his waist and her arms around his neck.

Kissing her, he walked her toward the bedroom.

And then her phone rang. She jumped down and scurried over to the couch, where she had left it.

"Is it him?" he asked.

"Worse. It's my dad."

She considered not answering it, but that was only going to delay the inevitable.

"Hi," she said shakily.

"We're having supper as a family tonight. I'd like you to be there."

Like that didn't sound at all ominous. "Can I invite Donovan?"

Donovan cocked his head at her.

"Of course. You owe that man a lot."

"I know."

"Six o'clock. Sharp."

"I know," she said, but he'd already hung up.

"What's going on?"

"We're invited for dinner tonight."

"Is that a good thing?" he asked.

"I can't imagine how it could be."

Her feelings were confirmed when they showed up a good half hour early and everyone was not only there, but already seated at the big dining room table.

Everyone.

The table was set and a trencher filled with steaks slathered with mushrooms and onions was in the middle. Her father had been grilling. There were large platters of steaming baked potatoes and sweet potatoes next to several slabs of butter and a dish of sour cream and chives. A crock of baked beans and a serving bowl overflowing with a garden salad comforted her that no matter how mad they were at her, at least they weren't going to starve her. Her mother went back into the kitchen and came back with steaming loaves of garlic bread.

"You've been busy," Emily said as she and Donovan took their seats.

"So have you," her father said.

"Frank, let's say grace." Her mother had them join hands and say a quick prayer.

As the food was passed around, her father's face grew more and more angry and she saw that he was building himself up to a terrible fury. Emily glanced at Kelly, who looked just as worried as she felt. Alissa sat between Kelly and Trent, blissfully unaware of PawPaw's disposition. Nate was digging into his food with gusto, while Janice played with her salad. Her mother was resolutely piling toppings on her baked potato.

The silence was deadly.

Her phone beeped a notification and she looked down at it. Five thousand dollars had been deposited into her checking account.

A text came through from Jules's number.

Tell Charlie I didn't know.

What the hell? She passed her phone to Donovan and saw him glance at it. He drew in a sharp intake of breath.

"Please turn off your phone at the dinner table," her mother scolded, giving her a reproving look.

Her father saw that as an opening to start his tirade, but Emily cut him off just as he was taking a deep breath to launch into her. "The money is back in my account."

It set him off his game and he faltered. Her mother slumped in her seat in relief and the tension eased around the table. It had been too much to hope for that her father hadn't filled in the rest of the family yet.

"That's good news," Kelly said faintly. She clutched Trent's hand. He gave her a reassuring smile.

"I know that I was stupid."

"Naïve," Janice interrupted. Emily hid a wince. In her mind, Janice was being helpful. In her father's mind, being naïve was worse than being stupid. He encountered stupid every day. Stupid could be educated. Naïve was weak.

"I should have been more cautious and spotted the warning signs. I let my eagerness for the project override my common sense and it was almost a disaster."

"Almost?" her father said, but he forked in a mouthful of rare and bloody steak. She looked away in disgust, but knew enough not to push her luck by complaining about it. This was his subtle way of punishing her. However, if he was eating, that was a good sign. He had a hard time holding on to his anger when his belly was full.

Emily ate a spoonful of her mother's baked beans and let the food comfort her. The brown sugar tasted like home. She knew that her mother had always made them vegetarian for her because Emily never liked the taste of pork, even as a child. She gave her mother a grateful look and accepted a piece of garlic bread from her.

"I'm sure Emily had a good scare and she's learned her lesson," Kelly said, helping to cut Alissa's steak.

Of course, that made her sound like she was Alissa's age. Emily wished her sisters would stop making her look like an idiot. Now, granted, she felt like one. But it was hard enough to earn her father's respect without using the old excuse that she was too young to know any better.

"It was nerve-racking for a few hours," she admitted. "And now I know that there aren't any shortcuts, so I'm going to hire the Sykes boys to clear the land and build a tower to test the wind speed. Then, if that's good, we'll go forward with the wind farm."

Of course, with five wind turbines instead of fifteen, it wouldn't be the grand plan she had hoped for, but it would be enough.

"What about that conservation museum you wanted to build?" her father asked.

Ah, that was a trick question. "I'd still like to see that happen. We've got some beautiful creatures on our land, but it's not a priority at the moment. We need to concentrate on making money, not spending it."

Her father eyeballed her to see if she was mocking him, but she wasn't.

"Hmm," he said noncommittally and went back to his plate.

Janice rolled her eyes and shook her head. "Well, that was easy," she muttered.

Nate nudged Janice with an elbow.

She rubbed the spot and frowned at him.

"The hayer is back up and running and the mechanic finally got the parts in so we don't have to jury-rig the ATVs," Nate said.

Emily was surprised to see he was looking at her instead of her father when he said that. "That's a relief," she said.

"Why are you telling her?" her father asked.

"It's her project."

"Hmm," Frank said again.

Emily counted that as a win. She mouthed *thank you* at Nate when no one was looking. He winked at her. "How's that sick cow?" she asked.

"Pete gave her a round of antibiotics. Should be fine in a few days. We're keeping her isolated."

"Janice, you should look after her," Frank said.

"I will." Janice smiled. "She's a sweetheart."

"Don't get attached. We'll probably sell her at market."

Janice's face fell. It wasn't as if she didn't know they sold their cattle to be slaughtered, but like Emily, she didn't like it. If there was a way to make money selling vegetables, Emily would be all for it. And while they did have a large garden, it usually only produced enough to feed them. If they had a bumper crop, they would contact the local CSAs or restaurant and negotiate a deal or two. If they could just get ahead of their bills, they'd be all right.

Emily got another text message from an unfamiliar number.

"Emily, I said turn that off." Her mother frowned.

Tell my son to come and visit.

Emily shut the phone off. But not before Donovan saw the text.

Chapter Eleven

"YOU DON'T HAVE to go with me," Donovan said. In fact, the farther away she stayed from his father, the better. He was going because it was apparent that the promise of money wasn't going to stop his father from butting into his life.

"Oh no, you stuck with me through that dinner and dessert last night. I owe you."

"Sneak away tonight and we'll call it even." He smiled and ran his finger down her cheek. He had been hoping that she'd have come over last night, but with everyone around, it probably was hard to get away.

"I was planning on it anyway, but I'm not letting you do this alone." And to prove her point, she got in his truck.

"It's a four-hour drive there and back."

"Then we better get going," she said. "We can stop on the way for snacks."

"This isn't a road trip," he said, exasperated. But because he wanted to be there before noon, he couldn't waste any more time arguing. "Where did you tell your parents you were going?"

"I didn't. It's none of their business. Besides if they need me, they have my cell phone number."

"Have you ever been inside a prison before?" Donovan started the truck and headed out of the ranch. He had planned on this being a grim and shitty drive, but he had a feeling Emily wasn't going to let that happen.

"Have you?"

"No, but you should probably leave your purse in the truck. They're going to frisk us and we'll need to go through a metal detector."

"Don't worry, I left my shiv behind."

"I'm sorry I got you involved in this. I should have never even mentioned my father to that asshole. I was just so sure he targeted you because of me."

She put a hand on his arm. "It's not your fault. As far as I'm concerned, it's over. I notified the bank not to accept any more wire transactions or to wire anything out without me providing a passcode for approval. I'm safe. And I got my money back because of you. Too bad I couldn't gain back the strides I'd made with my father thinking I wasn't a baby anymore."

"You did all right. You held your own. You did the right thing by admitting you made a mistake and then accepting the consequences. Do you think he never made a mistake?"

Emily snorted. "I experienced a bunch of them."

"There you have it."

"I just want him to take me seriously. I want all of them to."

"They will. They have to see that the girl who went to Africa grew up into the woman who came back. You'll show them. Just keep on doing what you're doing."

"I lost a lot of time being such a brat with your hunting tours." She stretched over to lean her head on his arm.

He gave her a brief hug, before putting his hands back on the wheel.

"It was just so easy to slip back into old habits. Thanks for putting up with me."

He shrugged. "I know it couldn't have been easy for you."

"About as easy as being a vegetarian in Texas." Emily straightened back up and he missed having her by his side. "But I learned to adapt. Tomorrow do you want to go to the Mustard Seed?"

"Sure, but you're not going to turn me into a vegetarian. I love my steak and ribs too much."

"Hey, if I can get my parents on board with meatless Monday, you'll come around eventually, too."

"I've got no issue with meatless Monday. Some of my favorite meals are meatless."

"Like what?" she challenged.

"Pizza."

"That's a good one."

"Eggplant parmesan."

"He likes Italian food." Emily pretended to be making notes in a journal.

"Your mom's apple pie."

"Yeah, I knew that one. Who doesn't?"

"I got to ask this. How can you not like bacon?"

Emily shuddered. "I hate bacon."

"And I thought you were the perfect woman."

"You did, huh?" She smiled in delight.

"You blew me in a tree stand. It doesn't get much better than that. But the bacon thing… Man, I don't know." He shook his head, teasing her.

"I could blow you in the truck."

Have mercy.

"I will crash into something if you do."

"You could park." She batted her eyes innocently.

"Maybe on the way back," he said. Definitely on the way back.

Emily was quiet for a while before she said, "I was about Alissa's age when I saw my dad and the farmhands slaughter a pig."

He winced. "Oh, honey, why weren't you playing with your dolls or something?"

"Because I was always playing in the dirt. Anyway, I never really liked the taste of meat anyway. Chicken was all right, until I realized I fed them every day. I never developed much of a bond with eggs, though. Still, it didn't feel right to eat something that I was taking care of. It felt like I was the witch in *Hansel and Gretel*, fattening them up. Of course, our chickens were egg layers. We didn't eat them. But it didn't make that much difference to me."

"It must have been hard to convince your parents you weren't just going through a phase."

"The phase has lasted nearly twenty years so far. But yeah, the cattleman's daughter not eating beef was a big joke for a while. I still think he's waiting for the day when I shout

April Fools' or something like that and devour a T-bone. I tricked him once, though."

"That doesn't surprise me."

"I eat tacos and enchiladas with a ground meat substitute. With the taco seasonings and all the toppings, you'd never know it wasn't beef."

"I would."

She shook her head in derision. "That's what they all say. But if you weren't specifically trying to taste the difference, you'd never know. I convinced my mother to serve him the soy crumbles instead of beef. He never knew. He even went back for seconds and thirds."

"What did he say when you told him about the switch?"

"He did his usual grunt and said..." She deepened her voice and said, in a convincing impression of her father, "I'll eat anything. Unlike some people."

Donovan nodded. That sounded like Frank.

"Of course, when he tried to turn the tables, it didn't end up so well."

"What do you mean?"

"He made my mother swap out my fake chicken nuggets with real ones. Or real-ish ones. I would have tasted it immediately if it had been my mother's fried chicken. These were store-bought so it wasn't apparent until I was puking my guts out for a few hours later that night."

"Ouch," he said, wincing.

"Yeah, it was a painful lesson for all of us. Let's just say he never tried to pull shit like that again."

"Living with him must have been a challenge, but I bet

you and your sisters gave him all that gray hair."

"I only hope so, because he deserves it." Emily smiled to take the sting out of her voice. "You should have met him before his health problems. He could outwork the youngest ranch hand we have. And when the rodeo came around? He was like a kid again. His greatest regret was not becoming a bull rider."

"He's tough enough for it."

"He wanted to do everything, but instead of getting good at one thing and then moving on, he signed up for all the events. He got on a bull that he wasn't prepared for and he got hurt real bad. I think it scared him because he never let an injury stop him from doing anything else. But he made sure Kelly, Janice, and I never made the same mistakes. I was the best barrel racer out of all of them."

"Of course you were."

"Kelly was a rodeo queen."

"I can see that."

"And Janice was just horse crazy. Only she rebelled from the rodeo and turned to English dressage."

"Janice strikes me as a rebel." Donovan grinned. "What about you?"

"Me? I'm the baby."

"No, that's Alissa," he said gently.

"Try telling that to them."

"They'll see it. Whether the wind farm becomes profitable or not."

"What if none of this works?" Emily asked. "What if my sisters and I try everything and we still have to sell the ranch?

What are my parents going to do?"

"They'll survive. They've got each other and you girls."

"I can't ever bring myself to imagine it."

"Then don't. You need to remain positive."

"I will if you will," she said, reaching out to hold his hand.

The trip was more pleasant with her next to him. They stopped for an early lunch, even though his stomach was in knots. But the pizza tasted better sharing it with her.

"Last chance to hang out in the car," he said. "I'm not even sure they'll let both of us see him."

"I'm coming in with you. Even if I have to wait in the lobby."

"Thanks." He kissed her sweetly on the lips, but then decided to linger because it felt so damned good.

"I'm pretty sure they've got security cameras set up in the parking lot." She giggled breathlessly.

"Let's get this over with so we can spend the rest of the day and night in bed." He kissed her again until she was shivery and gasping. Yeah, definitely all night long. His ardor cooled, though, the moment they showed their identification and were patted down.

"Wait here," a guard said.

Donovan led Emily to a cracked plastic chair, but he was too nervous to sit. He hadn't allowed himself to think about this moment since that infernal text came through. Hell, he hadn't even thought he'd ever see the old bastard again. What did you say to your own father who'd used you as a shield? Didn't that negate the man's right to call Donovan his son?

As he paced around the small room, he noticed a woman with a baby and a toddler and wondered what her husband did to land him in a medium-security prison. If his mother had survived, would they have visited Charlie together? Or would they have changed their names and started up again in another state. She always said she wanted to go to Hollywood and try her hand at being an actress. Or maybe they would have gone to Vegas. Nah, too much competition.

"Mr. Link?"

For a second, he almost didn't respond—he had been back to being Donny Lincoln. "Yeah," he said. "That's me." It was him. Donny Lincoln didn't exist anymore. Or maybe he only existed to one person.

"Just you."

He glanced back at Emily and she nodded at him in encouragement. "I'll be back in ten minutes," he said. He didn't care if they had a half hour. Charlie Lincoln didn't deserve any more of his time.

Donovan hated that his nerves were frayed. The guard led him to a circular table with two chairs. He had been expecting to sit across from him with solid plexiglass between them, talking on ancient phones. This was a little too real for him.

A door opened and a guard walked out with Charlie Lincoln. Even in the orange jumpsuit, he oozed confidence and quiet charm. A few of the guards smiled and nodded at him. He wasn't wearing ankle or wrist shackles either. Donovan watched way too much television, apparently.

"No touching," the guard warned when Charlie spread his hands out for a hug. He looked like a friendly grandfather figure. Donovan's fists clenched and he had to check himself from launching a punch into his father's smiling face.

"Can't I even shake my son's hand?"

"You know the rules," the guard said.

At least he didn't have them completely wrapped around his finger. Donovan hadn't stood up, and he stared at his father assessingly as he sat down. The guard went far enough away to give them privacy, but not too far.

"Hoping I palmed a file and would slip it to you?" Donovan drawled.

"After all these years, you think you could?"

Ten-year-old Donny would have puffed up with pride and told him of course he could. "What do you want?" he asked instead.

"I wanted to see my son. Fifteen years is a long time."

"About halfway through a thirty-year sentence," Donovan said.

Charlie leaned back in his chair and smiled at him. "I don't suppose you smoke?"

"No. You started?"

He shook his head. "No, but it's currency."

"I see. And you think I owe you for getting Jules St. John to back off?"

"A carton of cigs would go a long way to showing gratitude if I had done something like that."

"Any particular brand?" Donovan asked.

"Marlborough."

"I'll send it along. Are we done here?" He started to get up.

"Not just yet."

Donovan decided to hear him out. It would save him having to make any follow-up trips up here.

"Tell me about this hunting business of yours."

"It's temporary."

"Of course it is."

Donovan recognized the gleam in Charlie's eyes.

"I want a cut of it."

"Go fuck yourself," Donovan said politely.

"I could tell your landlord all about your past. Would that sweet little thing still stand by you if she found out who you really are?"

"She already knows." He chuckled. "Now we're done." He stood up.

"Wait. Wait. You can't blame a guy for trying."

"I blame you for a lot of things. My mother's death, most of all."

A spasm of something passed over Charlie's face. Normally, Donovan would have dismissed any show of emotion as contrived, but it was gone so quickly, Donovan had to wonder. If Charlie was playing him, he would have kept the regret and grief forefront. "Sit down. Please."

"No more bullshit," Donovan warned. He wasn't sure why he didn't leave. Maybe because there was still unfinished business between them.

"You broke the code when you ratted me out."

"You broke the code when you threw me in front of a bullet. What kind of piece of shit uses his son as a shield?" Donovan didn't mean to say that last part, because it made him vulnerable.

But instead of verbally pressing his attack, Charlie rubbed a hand over his face. "A stupid one. If I had to live that day again, we would have never gone to Barton's house. We would have dismantled the con and moved on. But I was so close to another million dollars, I let it blind me. And then I panicked. You never told me the son of a bitch had a gun."

"I never saw one. It must have been new."

"I thought the worst thing that could happen to me was going to jail." He shook his head. "I was a fucking greedy idiot."

"You'll get no argument from me. Why am I here? You could have asked me to send you the cigarettes in a letter."

Charlie leaned forward and lowered his voice to a bare whisper. Years of practice rushed back to him as he read his father's lips. Charlie breathed, "Are you running a con at the ranch?"

Donovan gave him a slight hand signal that they had used to mean no.

"Do you want to?"

Emphatic no.

"Are you serious about that girl?"

Donovan paused and gave another emphatic no. Whether he was or not, it was none of Charlie's business. "I'm moving on soon. I don't imagine we'll ever see each other again."

"I'm up for parole in a few months. I've been a real good boy in here. I'd like to come by and visit."

It was his worst nightmare and he forced himself not to react. "You should go visit Margaret's grave."

His father did better at hiding the reaction this time, but Donovan still caught it. Charlie was getting old. "I'm sorry," he said. "I'm so sorry."

Donovan frowned. "You've got to work on that. I like the ring of sincerity, but put a waver in your voice to sell it."

"You smug little shit. I am serious."

"You're sorry she died protecting me? Yeah, I kind of figured that, since you tossed me in front of the gun instead of her. I don't think Barton would have pulled the trigger if you had, but who knows? Something to think about." Donovan stood up for good this time and gestured to the guard that he was ready to leave.

"Fifteen years and you think I've never considered it?" Charlie said to his back. "I'll be in touch, son."

Not if he could help it.

"Everything go okay?" Emily said, embracing him.

Donovan looked back at the closing door and saw his father looking at them. Damn it. He hadn't wanted him to see Emily. Donovan glared at him until the door shut, blocking him out. He'd have to find out when the parole hearing was and send in a statement or something. There was no way in hell he was going to stand by while his father became a free man. The reason why Charlie had such a long prison sentence was because of his corruption of a minor child and the countless federal laws he broke.

Of course, why he hadn't been sent to a lower security prison yet was something Donovan wondered about, but didn't care to ask. He would have thought that a good lawyer would have gotten his father into a minimum-security prison by now. But maybe the reason Charlie was still here was…because he wanted to be. And that meant he was grifting from the inside.

Chapter Twelve

EMILY CONVINCED DONOVAN to stop at the Riverwalk before they went back because she knew neither one of them were going to feel up to cooking tonight. And they both needed coffee and a little romance to get their mind off the past few days.

"You're not going to make me take a boat ride, are you?" he groaned, stretching as he got out of the car.

"Maybe." She hugged him around the waist. "But I'd settle for a margarita the size of my head at one of those little tables by the river. We can watch the boats go by there."

"Sounds like a deal."

It felt good to walk around, after being cooped up in the car. Donovan was a good sport about window-shopping. He even bought her an Alex and Ani bracelet with an elephant charm because she squealed at how cute it was.

"I wasn't hinting that I wanted you to buy it for me," she said, turning her wrist this way and that so she could admire the little charm.

"I know. I wanted to get it for you. I like how it made you smile."

"You know what would really make me smile?"

"What's that?"

"Instead of hunting, how about we do a safari business?"

"Aside from the fact we live in Texas, not Africa?"

"You could still be all go-go-he-man hunter guide, except your guests would be shooting at the elk and deer with Nikons instead of thirty-aught-sixes."

"And the hogs? Will they take glamour shots with them, too?" Donovan asked dryly. "What's that phrase about putting lipstick on a pig?"

They held hands as they walked down the stone streets. It was a beautiful night out and even though they were bickering about hunting, Emily was enjoying herself.

"I think it would be a good idea. It's certainly more family friendly."

"Run it by your father. Maybe he can buy me out and bring in a safari guide."

"Do you have to talk about leaving?" she asked, her mood plummeting.

"Today you saw the very reason I have to go. At least you know what he looks like if he decides to show up. You just have to remember the key to figuring out if he's lying to you."

"What's that?"

"His lips are moving."

They followed the sound of the mariachi band until they got to Rita's on the River. They were lucky enough to get a table outside by the water.

"We'll start off with the chips and guacamole," Emily ordered when the waitress plunked down their Texas-sized margaritas. "They make it right at the table and it's so chunky."

"Works for me." Donovan took a deep sip of his margarita that had a Dos Equis bottle of beer upended in it.

"And for the entrée, vegetarian quesadillas."

"Same," he said around his straw.

When the waitress left, Emily said, "You don't have to get a vegetarian meal just because I am. I'm used to eating around carnivores. It doesn't bother me."

"I figured a few more extra vegetables a week won't kill me."

"Thank you for that," she said. "Not everyone is as willing to try new things." She stirred up her frozen peach margarita, fishing out the peach gummy candies to eat.

"That's not a real margarita," he pointed out.

"Says the man who has a beer in his drink."

"It's hitting like a real margarita," he said.

"Are you going to be all right to drive back?"

"I will be if we hang around long enough."

"I don't know if I want to wait that long," Emily said, licking the sugar off the rim of her margarita.

"I think I saw a vacancy sign on that hotel we passed."

"We're only a half hour from home," she said. "I can drive. Or are you one of those guys who won't let a girl drive his truck?"

"Sweetheart, you can drive whatever you like, as long as you get us to a bed tonight."

"That's a deal." She clinked glasses with him.

In the end, they passed on the second Texas-sized margarita and took their time eating their dinner. By the time the mariachi band played their last set, it was dark out and they were completely sober.

"Do you want to stay for the fireworks?" he asked.

"I'd rather go home with you and start our own," she said.

"Check please," Donovan called out.

She behaved herself on the car ride home, but she really couldn't wait to climb all over him. Of course, her parents were on the porch as they drove by. She waved and tried not to blush like a schoolgirl when Donovan drove past the ranch house.

"Are you sure you don't want me to drop you off?" Donovan teased.

"Nah, although you might get a talking-to from my father tomorrow morning."

"If I can handle my father, yours should be a breeze."

"You'd think that," Emily mused. But when she got out of the truck in front of Donovan's hunting lodge, she felt so free. She wanted to twirl around under the star-studded sky, so she did.

"I knew that was too much margarita for you."

"I feel free and I don't know why. It must be you. You make me happy." She held out her hand to him. "Come and dance with me."

"There's no music," he said.

"Then pretend."

He took her in his arms and they did a Texas two-step all around the parking lot.

"I'm not afraid of your father," she said. "Don't let him run you off."

"I don't want to talk about either one of our fathers right now. Or ever, really."

She nodded. "Let's go inside, cowboy. I want to make love to you."

Donovan led her by the hand into his bedroom. He kissed her softly at first, and she relished the lush feeling of having his mouth moving over hers. When he paused to lift off her T-shirt, she returned the favor.

"That's a pretty bra," he whispered, placing feathery kisses on her neck while he undid the clasp.

Emily wanted to give a witty reply, but his mouth was on hers again. He kissed her hard, while his fingers unbuttoned her jeans. Sliding her hands over the hard muscles on his back, she shimmied and stepped out of her panties as well. As he kissed down her neck, Emily helped him remove the rest of his clothes.

Pressing her naked body against his, she rubbed herself against his warmth and the velvet heat of his cock against her stomach. He walked her back to his bed and then dragged her down on top of him. She wanted to go slow, but she couldn't stop the frenzy of her hands and mouth all over his body. He was everything she ever wanted and if he thought she was going to give up on him—on all this—after three short years, he was mistaken.

"Come here," he growled and pulled her up so she straddled his face. Emily held on to the wall as his tongue shredded her control. He licked her fast, his hands hard on her hips keeping her in place as she wiggled on top of him.

"Donovan," she cried out as his relentless mouth kissed her intimately, sucking and pulling on her until she began to shake and gasp.

He groaned as she shivered in pleasure and the vibration tickled through her. Sighing and begging, she ground against him as a wave of joy and sensation flooded through her. Before she could recover, he pushed her gently back. Emily sprawled out, trying to catch her breath as he put on a condom. Eagerly, she opened her knees wide and he sank between him. Greedily, she guided him inside her, moaning as he drove deep.

He fucked her slow, each thrust long and hard. She wrapped her legs around him, accepting each pump of his hips by arching into them with a blissful sigh. He rocked against her, holding himself up on his forearms, while he kissed her sweetly.

Then he went faster. And she had to hold on to his shoulders, her nails digging in. With her head thrown back, she let out a throaty moan. Donovan's harsh breaths tickled her ear as he leaned in and whispered, "You're perfect." Then he held her arms over her head and drove into her with deep rapid strokes. Her second orgasm was cresting when he came hard. She was right behind him and they sank into a sweaty, shuddering pile of pleasure.

"You're pretty perfect, too," she said and kissed him until they fell asleep, wrapped in each other's arms.

Chapter Thirteen

DONOVAN WAS ON the phone with Otto Hendrick, one of his repeat customers. It was like a weird déjà vu conversation that slightly mirrored the safari one he'd had yesterday with Emily.

"You want me to get a what?" he asked, sure he'd heard the man wrong.

"A zebra."

"What the fuck for?"

"To hunt."

"It's a damned horse with stripes. Not to mention, I think it's illegal to do that."

"No, it's not. It's perfectly legal."

Deciding to humor the madman, he looked it up on the internet. At first, he thought it was a joke, but he got confirmation from several independent sources. "Son of a bitch," he said.

"See?"

Donovan couldn't even begin to imagine the utter shit show Emily would bring to his doorstep if he went to a zoo and bought a few zebras to breed for hunting. Not that he ever would. "I'm not willing to do that, Otto. I'll tell you what, though. There's plenty of places in Texas and it looks like in Florida, too, that will let you do that."

"Donny, you're throwing away money. People would pay you five grand to bag a zebra."

He didn't like being called Donny. It's what his father had always called him.

"You get elk, deer, turkey, and hogs, Otto. Maybe a javelina or two. Take it or leave it."

"Just think about it. We'll see you next week for elk. Stock up on that Rahr and Sons, would you?"

"That I can do, Otto. See you then."

He got off the phone, shaking his head. "Unbelievable." Zebras and giraffes. Emily would chain herself to one of them if she ever found out this was happening in Texas. Although, she probably knew. It wasn't, however, ever going to happen on the Three Sisters Ranch, that was for damned sure.

Emily was working with her father and Nate today with the cattle. She'd rolled out of his bed at an ungodly hour, but it was nice to watch her naked ass sway into the shower. And it was worth losing some sleep to have soapy shower sex. He hoped she was grinning at the memory just like he was.

Donovan took the ATV out through his hunting grounds. He spooked some hogs and thought he was in for some trouble. One chased him halfheartedly and then gave up when another male bellowed a challenge. He mentally noted the area so Otto and his friends could help clean up the menace. It was a good thing he wasn't on horseback today. He parked the ATV by the tree stand where he first saw the white elk. He hadn't seen her since that day, but he knew he was getting close. He'd go another five miles northeast this time and see what he could find.

He moved through the terrain silently, as always a little shocked that he felt so at home in the deep country. Growing up, he and his family had stuck to urban areas because that's where the money was. Donovan liked it here, damn it. He had thought that all his wandering around had made it difficult for him to be tracked down. But his father had found him anyway. He guessed he wasn't the only hunter in the family. Squatting down, he found deer tracks and something that suspiciously looked like it might be a cat print. But Texas pumas didn't come up this far.

He had hunted one in Washington after it had attacked a few hikers and killed a bunch of off-leash dogs. The poor thing had been diseased and near starving. It had been a mercy to put it out of its misery. But he took no pleasure in doing it.

The only other time he'd seen one was when he was hunting a rabid grizzly in Alaska. Donovan had been so focused on tracking the bear, he hadn't seen the cat on the rock ledge looking down at him. They had stared at each other while he had slowly backed away. He'd missed bagging the grizzly, but it had been worth it to pit himself against the puma and walk away unharmed.

He could have shot it. He had enough firepower to take down a six-hundred-pound bear. It didn't seem right, though. If it had charged him, Donovan would have had no problem pulling the trigger. But it had been content to laze on the rock ledge and watch the humans go by. Live and let live.

Fuck, that was all he needed—Otto and his jackholes getting wind there could be a lion around here. He took a picture of the print with his cell phone to compare it with one he'd search for on the internet. It definitely didn't have nail prints, so it probably wasn't a large dog. And a dog shouldn't be this far back either.

Staring around the area, he didn't even see a place for a big cat to hole up. Still, he'd better stick a game camera here, just in case. A thrill shot through him at the thought of a mountain lion. Emily would be proud that he didn't want to kill it. Not until it proved a threat to humans anyway. In his experience, if you left the puma alone, it left you alone.

Donovan unslung his rifle from his shoulder, just in case. After another few miles, he was about to give up when he heard the barking noises elk make, followed by a long bugle with an elk-y chuckle at the end. It was a little late in the season for mating, but not out of the question. The last freaking thing he wanted to do was get in the way of two bucks, though. There wasn't any high tree coverage either.

But he'd come this far, he might as well check it out. He didn't think it was the same herd that he was planning on bringing Otto's group to. Staying downwind, he circled the area and found a large rock that he could climb to get a better look. Slinging his rifle over his shoulder, he got a toe and finger hold and hoisted himself up. It was slow going, but he managed to pull himself up and sat on top of the rock.

Son of a bitch, there she was. Fumbling for his cell phone, he zoomed in the best he could and snapped pictures of her. She had a few suitors trying to impress her and a couple more approaching her. Of course, there wasn't a damned cell signal out here. At least now he knew where she was and he could set Kelly up on the rock for her pictures. If worse came to worst, he could leave a salt lick or two down there.

Climbing carefully down, his face hurt and he realized it was from grinning so much. How the hell was he going to leave here when his lease was up? He drove straight to the ranch house and knocked on the door. Sarah answered.

"Donovan, come on in. What brings you around?"

"I saw the white elk. I've got her on film." He pulled out his phone and showed her.

Sarah marveled at the picture, making him show it twice more. "Look at the size of her. I'd love to see her up close."

Nodding, Donovan accepted his phone back from her. "I think we can arrange that. I know Emily's not back yet, but I sent it to her once I had signal. I'm not sure she has signal where she is either."

"Probably not."

"That's what she really should do—put a cell tower on the land," Donovan joked. But the smile slid off his face. Why the hell not?

Sarah seemed to have the same thought. "I'll mention it to her."

"Couldn't hurt to look into it."

"Why don't you go show those pictures to Kelly. She and

Trent are up at the school. She's doing candid photos for some of the students."

"Will do." He turned to leave, but she stopped him when she cleared her throat.

"Donovan, what are your intentions toward my daughter?"

Oh boy.

"Would you believe me if I said my intentions were pure?"

"Do I look like I was born yesterday, son?"

He had to swallow hard for a moment. It had been a long time since a woman his mother's age had called him that. "I think the world of your daughter, Sarah. I think you guys don't give her the credit she deserves for growing up into a smart, fierce woman."

"Don't hurt her," she said.

"You first." He nodded his head at her. "Ma'am."

Donovan could feel Sarah's gaze on the back of his neck as he turned and left. Feeling like he'd dodged a bullet, he hopped back into the ATV and drove up the driveway to Trent's rodeo school. He pulled up to the building and saw Kelly taking some pictures of a group of students in the practice pen. The high school kids were practicing putting a bull into the chute and some were in the pen acting as bullfighters. Trent was with a nervous-looking boy who kept wringing his rope in his hand. It looked like they had their hands full. He should come back later.

Billy King, Trent's manager, was leaning up against the side of the school. He was talking with Alissa, Trent and

Kelly's five-year-old daughter. She was dancing back and forth on one foot and her face was curled up into a scowl. She looked five seconds away from having a meltdown. Hopping down from the ATV, he headed over. Maybe he could offer to take her for a ride or distract her with the picture of the white elk.

"I want to ride the bull," Alissa said, stomping around Billy.

Billy tried to reason with her. "Maybe when you're older."

"Hey, guys," Donovan said, walking up to them. "Alissa, do you want to see something?"

"No," she said, crossing her arms.

"How about a ride around the ranch? I promise to go real fast."

Alissa considered that for a moment. "Okay."

Thank you, Billy mouthed and took her hand.

They settled Alissa in between them and took the ATV on a wide circle around the training school and the new house. However, as they rounded the far corner, Donovan saw a pack of feral hogs rooting around the new development.

"Shit," Billy said.

"Shit," Alissa said gleefully.

Donovan stopped the ATV and reached under the seat for his rifle. Stepping out of the vehicle, he quickly loaded it.

"Billy, why don't you drive Alissa back to the school?"

"Piggies!" she said and jumped down.

Billy tried to grab her and missed.

The feral hog charged.

Donovan sprinted for her and scooped her up and all but threw her into the ATV. "Go!" Without waiting to see if Billy complied, Donovan dropped to one knee and sighted the rifle down on the boar that was thundering toward him.

Behind him, the ATV's engine roared and took off like a shot.

Donovan's first shot stopped the feral hog's charge. The pack scattered. Whipping his head over his shoulder, he saw Billy driving back to the school. After noting that Alissa wasn't looking, he put the hog out of its misery. Standing up, he fired his rifle twice at a fleeing hog. But he didn't have a clear shot at the other three who had decided there was easier prey and had retreated as fast as their hooves could take them.

Blowing out a tense breath, he scanned the area through the scope of his rifle. The hogs were getting really bold to come in this close to the new construction. When he didn't see anything else threatening him, he lowered the rifle and then slung it on his shoulder. Unsnapping his belt sheath, he took out his skinning knife. Donovan was about to call back to the ranch house to see if Sarah could meet him out here to take it after he dressed the hogs when his phone rang.

"You okay?" Billy said, breathing hard.

"Yeah," Donovan said. "Is Alissa all right?"

"She's fine."

"She wasn't scared?"

"No. She didn't even realize what was happening."

That was good. But someone was going to have to tell

her that feral hogs weren't piggies. They were dangerous. Before Donovan could mention this, Billy said shakily, "Thank you for saving my granddaughter."

Donovan was at a loss for words.

"Your what?" he heard Trent say on the other side of the phone.

"I'll talk with you later." Billy hung up the phone.

Billy had been with Trent all through his professional bull-riding career. And after Trent's accident and retirement, he still hung around as a business partner. Apparently, there was more to it. Although, he supposed Billy could have meant that since he had taken care of Trent for most of his life, he considered Alissa his granddaughter. Shaking his head, he called Sarah and she agreed to meet him with a cooler for the meat.

After dragging the other hog up to where he had shot the alpha, he was covered in sweat and gore from prepping the meat by the time Sarah got there. But Sarah didn't even blink and had brought extra water to drink and clean up with, along with some towels that would only be good for rags after this.

"Kelly called and told me what you did." Sarah hugged him hard once he had washed off.

Since he had taken off his shirt, it was a little awkward, but he patted her on the back. "Alissa wasn't in any danger," he lied.

Sarah snorted. "The hell she wasn't. You take down every last hog you see. Do you hear me, Donovan?"

"I hear you," he said.

"Trent wants to talk with you, too. I'll give you a ride back."

Donovan wished he had a shirt to put on, but once they were back in the rodeo school, Trent tossed him a school T-shirt.

"Thanks," Donovan said, appreciating the clean cotton.

"Thank you for dinner," Sarah said. "You'll be joining us, won't you."

It wasn't a question.

"Yes, ma'am," Donovan said, and shared a quick grin with Trent.

After she left, Trent's smile turned into a grimace and he eased into his chair.

"How's the leg?" Donovan said. Trent was still recovering from riding Corazon del Diablo for the huge purse that had given the Three Sisters Ranch some breathing room.

"I've had better days." He closed his eyes. "I don't know what I would have done if something had happened to Alissa."

"She's was fine. Billy was with me. He's the one who got her out of there."

"We heard the shots," Trent said. "But I didn't think anything of it until Kelly took off running as Billy pulled up in the ATV. Alissa was so excited and chattering happily and Billy just looked green."

"How's he doing?"

Trent rolled his head around on his neck. "What a day."

"You okay?"

"I found out Billy is my dad today."

"Oh." Donovan wasn't sure what to make of that.

"I never knew who my biological father was. After Alissa came into my life, I took a genealogical DNA test because I wanted to see if I could maybe track down my biological father. My mother had told me he was a bullfighter she never saw again. But it turns out that wasn't the case."

"Why did she lie to you?" Donovan wondered what the scam was. Why pretend that Trent's father was someone else? Was she extorting money? Unfortunately, those weren't the type of questions you could ask someone. He and Trent were friends, but more in a *have a beer once in while* friendship, not the *share deep, dark personal secrets* type. Although that could be where they were headed now. He wasn't sure how he felt about that. If he got too attached, it would just make leaving harder. Still, for three years, he could have a normal life. The last time that happened, he'd been in high school. And look how that ended up.

"I wish I could ask her. She died when I was a kid."

Donovan didn't mean to react, but something must have caught his attention because Trent said, "What?"

Clearing his throat, he said, "I lost my mom when I was a kid, too."

"Sucks, doesn't it."

Donovan nodded.

"You want a beer?"

"Shit yeah."

Trent winced as he got up and Donovan felt like a fool. "No, sit. I'll get it."

Waving him back to his seat, Trent said, "I've got to

move or I'll stiffen up and it'll be worse." He opened the fridge and handed Donovan a cold bottle.

Donovan tanked half of it before realizing he probably should have eaten something first. He'd been too excited about the white elk to remember to grab a sandwich and then, after dressing the hogs, he was still coming down from the adrenaline.

"I hadn't received the DNA test results back yet," Trent said. "But Billy obviously thinks it's true. He never told me he suspected it. My own father was right next to me for my entire life and I never knew." Trent shook his head. "I don't know how to feel about that."

"Did he treat you right?"

Trent looked at him in surprise. "Yeah, he treated me like I was his own son."

"I'm not seeing the problem." Donovan took another swig of his beer. "My old man is in prison for being a grade-A piece of shit."

Trent winced. "Sorry about that."

"I'm not. I hope he rots there. Billy always struck me as a nice guy. Did he love your mother?"

"He says he did. He says she wasn't the type to settle down, and from what I remember, that was true. When she wasn't drunk, she was heading that way to one party or another. From one man to another." Trent sighed. "It makes sense that she didn't know who my father was. I just can't figure out why she wouldn't tell me it was Billy. If it could have been anyone, why tell me it was a bullfighter she never saw again?"

"What does Billy think?"

"He refuses to say anything bad about her. But I'm wondering if she tried to get some other bull rider or bullfighter to pay child support."

Sounded reasonable to him. Follow the money. "Did she ever get any?"

"Billy wouldn't say. But it explains a lot about how he treated the women who claimed they'd had my baby."

Donovan nodded. Alissa was Trent and Kelly's little girl, but Trent hadn't known about that for most of Alissa's life because of Billy. "Are you happy that you know Billy's your biological dad?"

"Yeah, I mean he's been acting the part all these years and Alissa adores him. But I wish I'd known when I was a dumb kid that he was my father."

"Hindsight's a bitch." If Donovan knew then what he knew now, he would have tried to convince his mother to leave Charlie. Although that probably wouldn't have worked. She believed in Charlie's bullshit. She thought Charlie was her ticket to the good life. Instead, he had been her ticket to the afterlife.

"I'm sorry for getting so heavy about this. But after the close call with Alissa and Billy blurting out that he's her grandfather, I've been thrown for a loop. What had you originally come over for? Before the hogs?"

Donovan finished his beer, trying to swim out of all the memories of the past this week had dredged up. He was getting sleepy. The late night, the strenuous hike, the excitement and the emotion topped with the fast beer was sapping his energy.

"I found the elk. The white one." He pulled out his phone and showed Trent.

"Wow. I've never seen anything like that before."

"Why don't you hang around and show Kelly when she's done putting Alissa down for her nap?"

"Can I borrow your couch?"

"It's lumpy."

Donovan hid a yawn behind his hand. "I could stretch out on the floor mats."

"Be my guest. I'm going to drink a little more."

"Well, I can't let you drink alone."

And that's how Kelly found them, half passed out and staring blearily up at her. "I found her, Kelly," Donovan said and handed her his phone before his eyes shut.

Chapter Fourteen

EMILY WAS EXCITED to go on safari to see the white elk, even though Donovan was against calling it a safari. That's what it was and she got to share it with her sisters and the man she was falling in love with. It was hard to keep her heart guarded when every day was an adventure and every night was a dream come true.

She couldn't stop smiling and she knew it was only a matter of time before Donovan realized that they had just as good of a shot making money doing these nature safaris as he did with his hunting parties. Especially if there really was a puma, in addition to the white elk in the area. Of course, Donovan's trail camera hadn't provided any evidence that there actually was a large cat prowling around. It was still exciting to think she might see one up close—preferably from the safety of the truck.

It was finally a nice enough day that Kelly felt she could get some decent photographs. Unfortunately, Emily was roped into carrying the gear. She wasn't sure that they needed both Nate and Donovan armed with rifles. That was overkill in her opinion, especially with all the noise the trucks were making. Nate had Kelly and Janice with him in his truck, and Emily and Donovan had all the gear in Donovan's.

"Too bad we don't have a tree stand all to ourselves," she said, running her hand suggestively up his thigh.

"That would be fantastic, but all there is down there is a big rock. I wouldn't trust building a stand or a blind with all the elk rutting and the feral pigs in the area. Timber." Donovan made a crashing sound and mimed a tower falling over.

"This would be a nice safari."

"This isn't Africa. I'm not getting giraffes and zebras."

Emily rolled her eyes. "That's ridiculous."

"I'm glad you think so," he said under his breath. "Besides, if no one is here to thin out your hogs, there's not going to be enough forest left to support any other type of wildlife."

"Those hogs are a real cramp in my ass," she said.

"You and me both. But they're good eatin'."

"Gross," she said, without any anger. She knew he was just teasing her.

"Besides, no one is going to spend three hundred dollars a day to ride in a busted-up truck over ruts and foliage, hoping for a glimpse of Ghost."

"Perhaps not, but we could bring more people in to make up the numbers." Emily wasn't sure how yet, but she was working on it. If they could get the wind turbines in and the cell tower, they might be able to lease a Humvee or something to make the safari a little more exciting to book.

"I think you're overestimating the interest in a white

elk."

"Maybe." She didn't want to get into an argument about it. Not until she was able to research it properly. Emily just had to make sure today was fun and exciting. Donovan would see that there was money to be made from not killing animals.

"Did you look into the cell tower?"

She let the change of subject pass. She'd circle around to it again. "Yeah, I've got some credible leads. It could bring in about a thousand dollars a month, but they pay for everything. We just lease them the land."

"What's the catch?"

"It's got to be an exact fit for what they're looking for and it's a twenty-five-year lease."

"Hopefully you'll still be here to reap the benefits."

"I hope so. It'll pay a bill. And every little bit counts. I have a real surveyor team coming in to do a wind test once the Sykes brothers clear out the land." They had been complaining about seeing feral hogs, too, but the heavy machines kept them at bay. According to Mike Sykes though, he was "afraid to take a piss."

She should really tell Donovan to hunt around there. It would keep his crew this weekend away from the elk and the risk that they might see Ghost and try to take her head for a trophy. They liked hog meat. Bacon for everyone. Emily made a face. Now she was grossing herself out.

They parked by Donovan's cat camera and divided up the equipment. Since Donovan and Nate needed their hands free for their rifles, that meant that she and her sisters were hauling the gear. They hiked to the rock that Donovan had set up as a base camp. He had brought a ladder to make climbing it easier.

"I'll go first," Donovan said. "Nate, keep an eye out. There are hog tracks all over here."

"Here bacon, bacon, bacon," Nate crooned softly.

"Ugh please, no," Emily grumbled, following Donovan up the ladder.

The top of the rock wasn't big enough for all of them to sit comfortably, so after Janice handed up the equipment, Emily and Nate took up watch at the bottom of the rock.

"We'll switch in about an hour or so, sooner if we catch sight of Ghost."

"Maybe we should walk around and look for her?" Janice suggested.

"Don't split up," Donovan warned. "If you see her, both of you come back and tell us. Kelly can decide if she wants to wait for her to come to us or if she wants to do an action shot in the woods."

"Why not both?" Kelly said, adjusting her large-brimmed hat so the sun wasn't on her neck or face.

"Whatever you want."

After about two hours, Janice and Nate came back and Emily and Donovan took a turn walking around. They went in the opposite direction to see if they could flush out the elk.

"It's a waiting game," Donovan said, as they trudged up a hill.

"Is that why hunters sit around drinking all the time?"

Emily asked.

"When we're out in the field like this, we don't drink. Live ammo and booze don't mix."

"What if they're chilling in the tree stand?"

Donovan shook his head. "I don't get that. If you're going to sit and drink, stay on your porch. My insurance doesn't allow them to drink with rifles. However, I know that they sneak a few beers in the tree stands."

"It's all fun and games until someone gets shot," Emily said. Bunch of redneck yahoos. "Why don't you kick them out when they break the rules?"

"I've got insurance."

"Donovan," she said exasperatedly.

"It's the hunter's code. We watch out for each other. Accidents happen and we know the risks. I wouldn't take out anyone I thought was reckless or dangerous, so don't worry."

"Guns and alcohol don't mix. Add in some testosterone and it's a free-for-all."

"It's not quite as exciting as you're making it out to be. Most of the time they fall asleep in the blind. I personally can think of better things to do all alone in a tree stand." He grinned at her.

"Speaking of which, can't we just go back to the truck and make out?"

"Tempting offer," Donovan said. "I am going to miss you this weekend. I've got a full house of hunters again." He hooked an arm around her waist and kissed her.

She got little flutters in her stomach and a languorous warmth spread through her. This was nice. Emily was getting used to having him around. It should bother her, but in quiet moments like this, it was perfect.

"Are your guys going to come out here?"

"Not here exactly. I don't want them to stumble across Ghost."

"But you don't even know where she is. You could find her herd by mistake."

"Like I said before, I'll have them sign waivers that she's a protected species."

"And they call me naïve," Emily said.

They walked on another mile before they heard the rifle shots. "Was that Nate?" she asked.

"I think so. Don't run. It'll all be over by the time we get back anyway and if he's shooting at hogs, we don't want to run straight into them."

"I hope they're safe."

"The hogs?" Donovan asked.

"No, my sisters and Nate."

"As far as I know, the hogs can't climb ladders, not yet anyway. But they're evolving. They're not as afraid of humans or rifle shots anymore."

"What if it was the puma?"

"There was no sign of a big cat with the exception of that one print that could have been anything. No cat would take on three humans who had the high ground."

"So it's hogs, then?" she asked, trying not to worry.

"That'll be my guess, and we're more in danger from them than Nate and your sisters are. Of course, with all the racket, we should just call it a day. We're not going to see—"

He cut off at the sound of distant thunder.

Looking up, Emily saw there wasn't a cloud in the sky.

"Shit, we need to get some cover," he said.

"Is that a stampede?" she asked.

"Yes. And it's not your daddy's cattle. Let's go up this way. Now is the time to run." Grabbing her hand, he took off toward higher ground. The sounds of hoofbeats were getting louder and she only hoped that they were out of the path of the herd. They were coming fast and hard, as if something was chasing them. They wouldn't have been this spooked by a few rifle shots. They would have scattered, not run in what sounded like blind panic.

"Faster," he urged, and she saw a tree in the distance they might get safely up.

They reached the trunk and he knelt on the ground and laced his fingers like a stirrup. "Can you reach that branch and hoist yourself up on it if I give you a little toss?"

"Why do I need to?"

"Can you?" he said urgently.

"Yes." She stepped on his hand and half jumped and was half pushed up to grab at the branch. Her arms were shaking. She hated doing pull-ups, but she managed to haul herself over the thick tree branch. Catching her breath, Emily straddled it and then peered down at Donovan.

"What are you doing? Get up here."

He had his back to the tree and his rifle out and pointed. "We need to get walkie-talkies or something with range. Any chance you've got a cell signal?"

"No, damn it. But if my deal goes through, we will by

the end of the year."

"Hopefully we won't still be here," he said.

"You think it's the puma, don't you?"

"It could just as well be Bigfoot with the odds that it's a puma."

"Then why am I up here in a tree and you're down there?"

"I couldn't risk the time it would take me to get up the tree. I need you to be my eyes. Let me know if anything is coming."

"I don't like this," she said, but scanned the distance. "What am I looking for?"

"Movement. Not necessarily fast. If it is a big cat, it's going to be stalking slowly. We shouldn't be its target, though."

It was hard to hear him as the sounds of hooves got louder. Then she saw the elk. Now that they weren't in danger of being trampled to death, it was a majestic sight. She didn't see Ghost among them, though. Then they both heard the roar of a truck's motor.

"What the hell?" she said. A souped-up, off-road truck followed the herd. It was red and had large floodlights attached to the top. Usually a rig like that went out at night and flashed the floodlights to make the deer freeze. It made for easy shooting. Fucking cowards.

"Poachers," Donovan said, with the same disgust she felt in his voice.

More rifle shots reached them.

"Not on my land," Donovan said and aimed.

"Are you going to shoot them?" She gasped.

Donovan's first shot took out one back tire. He dashed across the hill and went flat on his stomach and took out the other back tire. The truck seesawed to a skidding halt.

"Stay in the tree," Donovan said. "I only want them to see me if they start looking."

Emily pressed herself back against the trunk, trying to make herself invisible.

Three men jumped out of the red truck and stared at the damage done to the tires. Donovan kept low, his rifle sighted on the men, but his finger off the trigger. Emily knew he'd hit the tire with a high-caliber round. It would have shredded the rubber. Would they realize Donovan had shot it out or would they think it blew on its own?

So far, they hadn't figured it out, but they only had one spare. Emily waited in the tree while they put the spare on one side of the car, but saw that they didn't have any idea what to do next.

Movement attracted her attention out of the corner of her eye. Hogs. They were shuffling toward Donovan's position.

"Donovan," she growled, hoping her voice didn't carry too far.

He looked over at her and she pointed. He pushed himself to his knees and saw the hogs. Standing up, he reloaded two more bullets into his rifle with quick, efficient movements. Would they catch his scent or was the wind blowing the other way? She jumped when his rifle cracked.

He wasn't giving them the chance to notice him. Donovan calmly worked the lever on his rifle back and fired again. Flip, fire. Flip, fire. Flip, fire. In the relative silence, the three men below them where shouting things like "What the hell is that?"

"There's two more," Emily cried, watching the hogs leap over the bodies of the larger ones that had been in the lead. Why weren't they running and scattering? These hogs truly weren't afraid of anything.

He calmly reloaded two more bullets. They were almost to him. Donovan took his time, aimed, and fired. The screaming of the hogs dying on the ground almost made her throw up. She closed her eyes and the last shot sounded louder somehow.

"Gentlemen," Donovan roared, attracting the attention of the poachers. "You are hunting on my land. But I think we can come to an agreement here."

"Wait. What?" Emily pried her eyes open and then decided she didn't want to see the carnage.

"I'm listening," one of the men shouted up at them.

"I've got seven hogs up here that you can have. But you're going to have to pay me what I charge hunters to take them out here and bag game." Donovan swiftly and quietly reloaded five bullets.

"How much are we talking about?"

"Three hundred dollars. Each of you."

"We don't have that kind of money on us."

"I'm sure you can get it. If not, sell the meat," Donovan said. "Of course, if you don't, I'm going to have to press charges of trespassing and then no one is happy."

"How do you know we just won't take the hogs and run?"

"Because I've got your license plate number and video of you jacking elk on my property."

She knew he was bluffing, but hopefully the men down there didn't know it. She heard Donovan moving and she pried open one eye. He was going down there and leaving her up here with the dead hogs all around the tree.

"We got a deal? Or do I shoot out your other tires?"

"These tires are expensive," one guy complained.

"So is jail time."

"How are we going to get back with only three tires?"

"For an extra convenience fee, I'll drive one of you back to a garage to get another tire while the other two of you dress the hogs and put them in the truck."

"How much?" the complainer asked.

"Tack on another hundred so it's an even thousand you owe me, and we'll call it even."

"Don't negotiate with terrorists," she hissed.

"Deal."

"Oh, and don't come back here again unless you're a paying guest," Donovan added.

"Deal."

"What are you doing? You don't want them coming back here, paying guest or not." She was shaking with rage or fear, Emily wasn't sure.

Donovan leaned his rifle against the tree and held his arms up to her. "Come on, sweetheart, let's get you down from there."

Emily didn't think she could move, but she lay down on her stomach and dangled her legs.

"Drop. I've got you," he said.

She didn't have much choice—her legs and arms felt like rubber. True to his word, he caught her and set her gently on her feet. "I don't feel well," she said.

"Do you want to wait here while I get the truck?"

"No. We need to press charges." She held on to him in a death grip. She wanted him to carry her back to the truck. She wanted to be in her room in the ranch house far away from rifles and hogs and elk-jacking trespassers.

"It's handled. If it happens again, I'll call in the cops. Right now, it's a win-win situation."

"They could have killed Ghost," Emily wailed into his shirt.

"She wasn't in the herd they were chasing."

"How do we know they didn't kill her first? Maybe that's the gunfire we heard?"

"They wouldn't have left their trophy. Are you all right to walk?"

She pushed out of his arms. "I'm fine." Emily staggered a bit. "I'm fine."

But she wasn't fine. Not one damned bit. Her knees were shaking and she felt like she was going to throw up. The poachers could have killed them instead of the elk. They were trespassing and probably half drunk. Emily had always felt safe on her own land. Now she would always look over her shoulder and wonder who was out there.

"Where did you learn to shoot like that?" she asked, rubbing her arms. She felt cold and shaky.

"Girl Scouts," he quipped.

"Donovan, I mean it. You never missed. Not once. That's almost impossible."

"Not with the caliber of ammo I use. It's not a big deal. I spent a lot of time practicing. You just have to keep cool and take your time on the shot."

"You didn't have a lot of time. You killed seven hogs. Doesn't that register?"

"It's a little exciting." He flashed her a grin.

"Death excites you?" She stumbled down the hill away from him and then flinched away at the poachers from the red truck.

"How did you get here?" Emily demanded. Surely they hadn't been bold enough to drive down the ranch's driveway.

"We came through the state's lands." One of the guys pointed toward the west. "We didn't know we were on private property."

Emily bit her tongue before she went off on them. They weren't supposed to be running through state land with their truck chasing down herds of wild animals either.

When they finally got back to Nate and her sisters, she refused to ride with the poacher.

"What happened?" Kelly asked. "We heard all the noise."

"I'll explain later," Emily said shakily and made a beeline for Nate's truck.

Squeezed in between Kelly and Janice, it was a bumpy ride for Nate, but after Emily explained what had happened, no one complained. The off-road vehicle hadn't gone near where they had been. But there still hadn't been any sign of Ghost.

Janice put her arm around Emily and Kelly kept handing her tissues. Emily didn't know why she was crying—that was usually Janice's preferred method of handling stress.

"The hogs would have killed him, right?" she said between sobs. "But then he shot all of them like a demented Doc Holliday. He shot all of them. He was so cold. It was nothing to him. Then he gave the meat to the poachers. They're not going to jail." She shook with fury and with sadness. "These so-called hunters don't care about anything but their cheap thrills. We have to protect Ghost. We have to." She couldn't trust Donovan's judgment when it came to these assholes. He'd give them the benefit of the doubt.

Hunter's code, my ass.

"We will," Kelly soothed. "We'll find her again. I know we will."

If the hunters wanted to hunt, they could hunt hogs. Emily's mind quailed away from the thought of killing, but she had to toughen up and choose. She couldn't stop Donovan's hunts, but she could, at least, direct them.

Chapter Fifteen

THINGS WERE SHITTY with Emily, and not for the first time, Donovan wished Otto and his crew hadn't booked this weekend. But they had and they were already here. And Emily was still distressed about what had happened with the hogs and the poachers. He knew it was upsetting to her to see animals die, but the gang of feral hogs who weren't afraid of man, machine, or gunfire were not what he wanted to run into on a stroll through the woods.

Besides, the meat didn't go to waste and he got paid for it. He did feel badly that she was traumatized by it. Emily was just too kindhearted, but it felt like it had pushed their relationship back to where it was in the beginning when they were adversaries.

"Just leave me alone for a bit," she had said to him, so he gave her the space she needed.

Still, he missed her. Of course, maybe this was for the best. He was rapidly falling in love with her and their relationship had an expiration date. Getting his heart involved wasn't part of the plan. Of course, it wasn't that easy to ignore how wonderful she was—even if she was too tenderhearted.

Otto and friends arrived shortly before six and they had a barbecue with the ranch hands. The beer was flowing and everyone was having a good time telling stories. Then one of Nate's boys decided to tell the story of the white elk.

Son of a bitch.

"We've all seen her," the ranch hand said. "At one time or another. She's pure white and the size of a car."

That was a bit of an exaggeration. She was good-sized for a female, but she didn't weigh more than seven or eight hundred pounds.

Otto laughed. "I wasn't born yesterday, boy."

"Ask Donovan. He's got pictures on his phone."

"That right, Donny?"

He sighed. "I was going to show you it tomorrow. And you've got to sign waivers that if you see Ghost, she's off-limits."

"Show us your phone," Otto said. "I think you guys are full of shit."

"I can do one better." He went inside and got the digital picture frame that he'd loaded the video and pictures on to. It was only the size of a tablet, but it beat all of them crowding around him and his tiny phone screen. Donovan passed it to Otto and went back to finishing his dinner.

They must have played it back about five times before Otto looked up at him. "This is better than the zebra. I'll pay you five thousand dollars for her head. Hell, I don't even have to shoot her."

"No. She's protected. That's a condition of my lease." A verbal one anyway. "We are not allowed to hunt the white elk." Not that he was going to lead them to her anyway, but he wanted that to be clear.

"Donny, you're a terrible businessman."

"Be that as it may, Ghost and any other white elk you see are off-limits."

They grumbled about it, but in the end, what were they doing to do about it? After the fire was out and the beer was gone, they headed back into the hunting lodge and called it a night. They were going to get in the trucks at dawn and head out to bag what they could.

Donovan paused on the porch and looked toward the ranch house. He could just see the lights in the distance. He wondered what Emily was doing now. Walking back to his bedroom, he waffled about calling her. But she wanted some time and, truth be told, he didn't want to hear her bitch about the hunting party, so he put his phone to charge and went to bed.

EMILY COULDN'T SLEEP. Creeping out onto the porch, she silently closed the door so as not to wake anyone. She could see the lights of Donovan's hunting lodge in the distance. There had to be a way she could stop them from killing Ghost, or any of the other elk. She grudgingly accepted that the hogs were a problem and she wasn't a hypocrite. She knew if they just relocated the hogs, they would be killed off-ranch. It was more humane for Donovan to kill them with one shot than it would be for them to be terrified until they were slaughtered.

But the elk weren't hurting anyone. Nature was keeping their population in check.

She wished she didn't care for Donovan as much as she did. It would have been so much easier to hate him if he was a stereotypical hunter and just out for himself. But she saw how kind and protective he was. She would never be able to repay him for keeping Alissa safe.

If he hadn't shared his childhood with her, Emily wouldn't be feeling guilty that he would be moving on. He needed a home and a family and she could give him both. All she would have to do was accept that he made his living killing animals.

Only she just couldn't do that. She could compromise on the hogs, not because she wanted to but because there wasn't an alternative solution that would allow them to live. And the meat went to feed the hungry—if not her own family, then the local soup kitchens and restaurants. She wouldn't eat it, but the hogs wouldn't die in vain.

But with every gunshot, she cringed at the turkey, javelinas, deer, and elk that would senselessly die for someone's cheap thrills.

When she was in charge of the ranch, she could make those changes. But she wasn't, and hopefully her father would be around for a long time so she would have time to learn from him and maybe bring him around to her way of thinking.

Rubbing her shoulders against the chill in the breeze, Emily wished she could go to Donovan and convince him to change his clientele to people who would appreciate the beauty of nature instead of wanting to destroy it. He was everything she wanted in a man, and everything she hated at the same time. Fate had a sense of humor.

Emily took a step off the porch and paused. He was leaving after his lease was up. Every night she spent with him would make it more difficult to let him go. What had started out as something fun and casual had developed into something more. She thought he felt the same way, but she knew he would leave all the same. He may be a hunter, but Donovan was also a protector. He would leave to protect them from his father.

The power company was coming out tomorrow to take a look at the property for the wind turbines and surprise—they weren't charging her a dime to do it. If things went well, she could start construction on the first of the turbines by the end of the month. Emily needed to move forward for the sake of her family and the ranch.

But she wished that she could go back and have some more carefree zip-line adventures and wild tree-stand sex with Donovan before things had gotten so serious.

Chapter Sixteen

THE NEXT MORNING, Donovan split the group into two parties. He took two guys in his truck and told Otto to follow him with the other two guys in his truck. They drove back farther than Donovan had taken them before, but nowhere near the white elk rock, as he'd started to call it in his head.

He had gotten smart and bit the bullet, buying some high-end two-way radios. Donovan passed them out to the group. If they came up empty with elk today, they could always hit the whitetails that came at sunrise and sunset to snack at the automatic corn feeders he had set up. They parked the trucks and made sure that the ice chests were secure to store the meat in. He led them down to the blinds he'd set up along the area where he'd tracked the other herds and assisted in getting the men settled in them.

They'd stay here for a few hours and then move to another area. Donovan had set up a few salt licks there, so they may have better luck. As the hours passed by, the only thing they saw was a few javelinas and a couple of wild turkeys. The group decided to hold off on taking them so as not to scare off the elk. When it was time to move on, Otto and his group were itching to shoot something.

"Patience," he advised. "But if you want to take out the smaller game, be my guest."

They were hiking up an incline when they heard hoofbeats. "Hold up," Donovan said. It didn't sound like a herd.

There was a flash of white in the distance and Otto cried, "There she is."

"No," Donovan said, as Otto took aim.

He was too far away to stop him. Otto fired.

There was a very human scream. Donovan was already running in that direction. The panicked horse made high-pitched cries and fled, its hoofbeats thudding off in the distance.

Then he heard Emily shout hysterically, "Help me. Sunflower's been hit."

EMILY WAS BRUISED and scratched up from being thrown from her horse. She was bloody, but it was from Sunflower. She was barely aware that Donovan had scooped her up and was carrying her.

"Is she all right? I didn't hit her, did I?" Otto said, pushing in close.

Donovan shoved him back with his shoulder.

"He killed her," she cried.

"Sunflower ran away," Donovan said. "She's probably heading back to the ranch."

"You shot at me," Emily said, getting some sense back.

"Put me down." She wiggled to be free.

Donovan reluctantly set her on her feet.

"What the hell were you doing out in an active shooter zone, girl?" Otto said.

Donovan whirled and punched him in the jaw. Otto staggered back and would have lunged at him, but his friends got in the middle of it and held both of them back.

"Hogs," Emily panted. "They're all over the wind turbine site. I can't bring in the cell tower surveyor because they're menacing anything that comes near. I wanted..." She took in deep gulps of air. "I couldn't reach you on your phone. I thought..." She put a hand to her head. "I've got to find Sunflower." Emily's head felt like it had split open, but she couldn't find a wound and it was getting awfully hard to think.

"I'll take you back. Let me carry you to the truck." Donovan moved to pick her up.

"I'm fine." She staggered away from him. "You can't leave these madmen out here alone. They'll kill Ghost. They'll kill everything." Was she even making sense? She couldn't feel her tongue.

"You're more important," he said, reaching for her again.

"No. We all go. Or I'm not going. I'll make so much noise, you boys won't even catch a cold."

"This is bullshit, Link."

"You shot at my woman, Otto. You deserved more than a punch."

"Look, Neanderthals, pound your chests later. My horse could be dying," Emily cried. Her vision doubled and things got blurry.

"I'm real sorry about that," Otto said. "I thought you were the white elk."

"Which you were told you weren't allowed to hunt." Emily sagged against Donovan. "I told you. I told you. Men like these can't be trusted." It hurt to breathe.

"You watch yourself, missy." Otto pointed at her.

"Or what?" Donovan said between his teeth and would have gone after him again, but she tugged him away.

"Stop. Stop. Look, you can hunt all the hogs you want today or I can cuss you out until dark. And if my horse is dead, I may take a rifle to you myself. And if you think you can cut her up and send her to process for her meat..." Emily's voice sounded shrill and hysterical to her ears and she fought to shut up, but her head was pounding and every bone in her body ached. "I hate you. I hate that you have to kill things to feel like men. I hate that you have to destroy beauty. That you have to eat it. I hate it!"

Her legs gave out, and everything went dark.

Chapter Seventeen

EMILY WOKE UP in her own bed and for a moment, she thought it had all been a terrible dream. But then the pain hit her and she closed her eyes and whimpered.

"Take this," her father said. He handed her two tablets and put a glass of water to her lips.

"Sunflower?" she asked, trying to sit up.

Frank put the glass on the bedside table. "Easy there. Doc thinks you have a concussion."

"Why does my arm hurt so bad?" She looked down and saw it was in a cloth sling.

"You dislocated your shoulder when Sunflower threw you."

"Is she dead?" she asked, her voice shaking.

"She lost a lot of blood and you're not going to be able to ride her for a while, but Janice and Pete are taking good care of her. It scared the life out of us when she came back shot and you weren't on her." Her father's hands were shaking.

Emily reached out and held them. "I'm sorry for worrying you. Donovan's hunting party thought we were the white elk and shot at us."

"I know. He told us. You shouldn't have gone out there."

"I wanted to tell Donovan about the hogs."

"It could have waited until they came back for the day. You did it to screw up the hunt."

Emily tried to glare at her father, but it hurt too much. She hated when he saw right through her. "I thought it would be a win-win situation. They could bag all the hogs they wanted and keep away from the elk."

"I'm not saying that Otto guy was right. He could have killed you. He was a reckless shooter and Donovan is taking care of him."

"What do you mean?"

"I mean he kicked him and his party off the ranch and banned them. But you were wrong to go out there. You know better. I taught you better. You risked your life and I can't have that."

"I'm sorry, Dad."

"So am I. I told Donovan that he had to go."

"What?" Another blast of pain hit her as she tried and failed to get up. "Why? It's not his fault."

"Baby girl, I know that. He's a good man, too, which is why this is so hard."

"I didn't mean for this to happen."

"I know it. I should have seen it coming, though. I should have known you'd never give up your cause to protect the animals. I had thought you and he came to an agreement."

"We did. We compromised."

"But then you went back on that because you thought you were doing right and saving the great white elk."

"The hogs needed to be cleared," she said weakly, but heard it as the excuse she was.

"He's the one clearing out now. We mutually agreed to cancel the three-year lease. And once the ranch is sold, I'll make it right with him to reimburse him for the hunting lodge."

"Dad, you can't. We need that lease."

"I need you even more."

"We were barely making it before. I'm going to need time to get the cell tower and the wind turbines set up. We need Donovan. I need Donovan." She tried to get up again, but her body wouldn't respond. She tried to fight through the pain, but it only made it weaker. "Dad. Help me."

"You need to rest. You've got nothing to worry about. Your mother and I will take care of everything. We were wrong to put this on you and your sisters."

All her worst nightmares were coming true. They were losing the ranch because of her. "No, you weren't. We can do this. We can save the ranch."

"This ranch doesn't mean anything to me if you girls aren't around. It's not worth your life." He cupped her chin and kissed her forehead.

"Where's my phone? I need to talk to Donovan."

"He's busy right now. Let the man pack in peace. I'll make sure he comes up to say goodbye."

"I want to see him," she said, blinded by the tears in her eyes.

"Baby girl, you need to realize that you can't always get what you want." Her father's voice was kind and tinged with sadness. "Now, try to get some rest. We're going to need to wake you up throughout the night to make sure you're all right, because of your head injury. So rest while you can."

"I can fix this," she said. "I can."

"You need to concentrate on getting better."

"Are Janice and Kelly mad at me?" she asked in a small voice.

"They were worried about you."

"I'm sorry."

"I know." He put his hand on her forehead. It was warm and comforting. "I'm sorry, too."

Even without her parents checking in on her every few hours, she didn't get a lot of sleep. She played with the breakfast her mother gave her and only ate her toast because her mother hovered and fretted until she did.

Kelly played nursemaid around lunchtime and distractedly set up a tray for her across the bed. "What's going on?" Emily asked.

Kelly smiled at her. "The usual things. Cattle problems. Sunflower is playing up her injury for treats. I think if she gets any more peppermints from us, she'll have a sick stomach. But she's loving the attention. Do you want to go and see her?"

Emily's eyes flooded with tears. "Am I allowed out of bed?"

"The doctor didn't say you were bedridden."

She moved gingerly and she was still in a lot of pain, but

a few more Tylenol and a hot shower worked wonders. Kelly helped her get dressed and supported her as they went slowly down the stairs.

"Are you sure you're up to this?" her mother asked.

"Yeah. I might not be able to get back upstairs again, but so far, I'm moving."

"How do you feel?"

"Like I got run over by a bus."

"Don't overdo it," her mother said.

"We're just going to the barn," Kelly said.

"Be careful."

Sunflower was glad to see her, even though Emily only gave her some baby carrots and an apple. Janice was there and changed Sunflower's dressing and showed Emily her wound. The bullet hadn't shattered bone and it had missed the vital organs, but Sunflower had lost a lot of blood and had been in surgery to remove the bullet. They had been lucky. A few inches lower and Sunflower would have died. A few inches higher and Emily would have been hit instead.

Kelly helped her to the bench when she started to shake. They left her there while they did some chores around the barn. Emily was glad to be out of her bedroom, although she was tired. She took out her phone and called Donovan, and she was surprised when he answered. She was afraid he was mad at her and would have let the call go to voice mail.

"Hey," she said, her voice tremulous.

"How are you feeling?"

Emily almost started crying again when his voice was warm and kind. She didn't deserve that. "It hurts, but I'm in the barn with Sunflower."

"How's she doing?"

"She's back to her old tricks, but it's going to be a long recovery."

"How about you?"

"I'm all right. The concussion and my shoulder will slow me down for a bit, but not too long. Can I see you?"

There was a long pause and for a moment, she thought he would say no. "Sure. I don't want to tire you out, though. Do you want me to come by later?"

"No. I mean yes, if that's when you can get away. But I'd like to see you now."

"All right. Give me a few and I'll meet you at the barn."

It was an eternity, but she heard his truck pull up and when he poked his head into the barn, she wanted to run to him. But she could barely stagger to her feet. And then somehow, he was there and she was in his arms.

"I'm so sorry," she said.

"Shh, you've got nothing to be sorry about."

"Don't go. I can convince my father to let you stay."

"It was my idea."

She stiffened. "What? Why?"

"Emily, I'm falling in love with you and you know I can't stay. And you don't want me to."

"I do," she said. "I'm falling in love with you, too."

He kissed her sweetly. "Thank you for that. But we're too different. I'm a hunter. That's what I do. I like it. I'm good at it. And I believe in what I'm doing. That's the polar opposite of you and your beliefs. I don't want to worry that our fundamental differences will put you at risk like this. It's not worth it. I won't risk you."

"I'll be better. I'll change. We can make this work."

"I don't want you to change. You shouldn't have to change. I know this is a loss to the ranch..."

"I don't care about that right now. I care about you."

"I had an idea. I've got hunting insurance that covers this type of thing. I'll give you the information and you can file a claim. I won't fight it, but it should give you enough to get you through until you find another renter. Someone who fits your values a little better than me."

"Donovan, don't do this. I don't want you to go." She held on to him tight and he hugged her back.

"You don't need to be upset. This will work out. I'll come back from time to time and visit."

"Promise?" There was still hope, then.

"I'll check up on you. Just remember, if Charlie comes looking for me, you haven't seen me. And don't believe a damned word he says. And don't give him a nickel. Promise me."

She nodded. "When are you leaving?"

"Tonight."

"You don't have to go so quickly." She was losing him. He was slipping right between her fingers.

"The longer I stay, the harder it's going to be to leave."

"Where are you going?"

"I haven't decided yet. Maybe back to Alaska. I missed out on a grizzly bear the last time I was there. I don't suppose you want me to send you back a claw necklace?"

Emily couldn't help the shudder that went through her. He was being deliberately gross to make this easier on her. It would never be easy.

"I want to make this right. I've done nothing but fuck up since I got back from Africa. I've ruined everything and I don't know how to fix it." She looked up at him. "Can you tell me what to do?"

"Would you listen if I did?" He smiled to take the sting out of his words and reluctantly stepped away from her. "Take care."

"Donovan," she said.

He paused, but she couldn't think of anything to say that would make him stay.

"I know," he said.

He kissed her gently one last time and walked away.

Chapter Eighteen

EMILY WAS HAPPY for her sister, but miserable for herself. Kelly and Trent were in full-on planning mode for their wedding as a way to lighten up the gloomy atmosphere around the ranch. While Kelly was going to be a beautiful bride, she also had tinges of Bridezilla. They wanted their wedding to be held on the ranch and Kelly was searching for the perfect setting and background for her engagement pictures. Kelly and Trent's property would always be a part of the Three Sisters Ranch in all of their hearts—that is, until the rest of the ranch was parceled up and sold.

That was the current plan if things didn't work out with the wind turbines and the cell tower. It broke her heart, but she wasn't ready to throw in the towel yet. Janice and Kelly weren't giving up either, even if their parents had resigned themselves to it.

The feral hogs were becoming more of a problem. All the ranch hands had rifles on their saddles and it wasn't safe to venture out back in the woods. Emily wanted to see Ghost again, to see if she would bring them luck. But she wouldn't risk any of the horses and she didn't know the area back there as well as Donovan did.

It had been a couple of weeks since Sunflower had been shot and she missed Donovan like crazy. Sometimes she wandered around the hunting lodge looking for a trace of him. As she left the lodge today, she ran into her father walking up from the woods, a rifle in his hand.

"Dad," she said. "What are you doing here?"

"I'm trying to track down the sounder that all these hogs are coming from, but they keep splitting off. What are you doing here?"

"I thought I left something here," she said lamely. "Why are you walking?"

"The ATV broke down on me."

"Again? We need a new one."

"We need a lot of new things," he grumbled, holding his ribs.

"Get inside and sit down," Emily said, running to help him. "Let me get you some water. You shouldn't be doing this all alone."

"Don't fuss over me, baby girl. I'm fine."

He didn't look fine.

"What did you think you left over here?" he asked, accepting the large glass of water she gave him. He drained it in one long swallow and asked for another.

"My heart," she said under her breath. "Dad, I've been thinking," she said louder when she handed him his refill. "I was wrong about Donovan's hunting. I still don't like the idea of killing animals for sport, but I can see all the problems we've been having since no one is here to keep them in check. And while I don't eat meat, a few of the local soup kitchens have been calling because Donovan hasn't been making any deliveries lately. People are going hungry because of me."

He shook his head. "It's not your fault people are hungry."

"But I can make a difference here. I thought about all the good I was doing in Africa and I miss that. But I want to start in Texas. I want your permission to ask Donovan if he'll come back to the ranch."

"Something tells me you're not doing this for the good of the hungry people out there."

She smiled. "I love him, Dad. And I think he loves me."

"He better," Frank grumbled.

"I know we'll never see completely eye-to-eye on things, but I think we can compromise. I thought I could handle the hunting tour groups, but I can't. I told everyone it was fine, but it wasn't. It wasn't fair to him. And it wasn't fair to you guys. I really screwed up and now the ranch is worse off than before. I want to make it right. I know we can save the ranch from foreclosure if we all work together and Donovan is a part of that."

Her father regarded her thoughtfully. "I know you want to take over for me when I retire. You've been putting in the hours, but you have a long way to go."

"I know. And I'm willing to keep on learning. I'm going to make mistakes, but just because I do, that doesn't mean I'm not mature enough for the responsibility or that I should be patted on the head and forgiven because I'm the youngest."

He nodded and sipped his water.

"Just don't give up on me, Dad. And I won't give up on you. It'll be hard work, but the Sullivans will make this happen. We just have to hold out until the wind turbines turn a profit."

Part of his mouth quirked up in a smile. "If you can get Donovan to come back, it's all right by me."

"I'll not only get him back, I'll make him stay here, too. No three-year leases this time. Twenty-five-year—minimum."

Frank shook his head. "He'd be better off marrying you."

"I'll accept that as well."

DONOVAN DIDN'T KNOW why he hadn't left Texas yet. It had been almost a month. Maybe because winter in Alaska wasn't appealing. Of course, that didn't explain why he wasn't off to California instead. But then Emily called and asked to meet him at the Mustard Seed. And he realized why he was still hanging around.

He loved her.

He was early, so he fiddled with the radio trying not to relate to every sad love song the station played. After an eternity, she got out of her Uber ride and headed toward the truck. Donovan leapt out and met her halfway.

"How are you feeling?" he asked, bringing her in for a hug and a kiss. And if the kiss lasted longer than was polite in a social setting, he didn't give a fuck.

"Good as new," she said breathlessly. And then she stood up on her tiptoes and kissed him again. He wasn't sure they were going to make it to the restaurant. He could spend all day kissing her in the parking lot. But then her stomach growled and they broke away, laughing.

"Your mother hasn't been feeding you?" he teased.

"Don't tell her, but the Mustard Seed makes better vegetarian meals. She tries, though." Emily slipped her hand into his while they walked to the restaurant. It felt like coming home. Maybe he could find a ranch hand job and stay in the area. It wasn't as if he couldn't do the work. It was how he'd survived after being emancipated. He could make ends meet by hunting. What Emily didn't know wouldn't hurt her. He wasn't ready to give her up just yet.

They sat down and Carrie brought them their menus and beers. Emily wound up ordering half the menu again, and he tried the spaghetti with meatless balls. He didn't have high hopes for it, but he liked seeing her smile when he ordered something different.

"I have a proposition for you," she said with a cute little smile.

"You should have told me before we ordered. But it's been a while, so I bet we can go out to the car and be back before lunch is served."

"Tempting," she said. "But I want to take my time with you."

"Then you should have told me in the parking lot, and I would have brought you back to my place."

"I was hungry, but we could go there after lunch."

Heat flooded through him at her shy words and he wanted to start in right there, right now. But he could be patient. He was a hunter after all. But she wasn't prey. In fact, the way she was looking at him was damned near predatory.

"But that wasn't the proposition I meant."

"Okay," he said. As long as they were going to bed after this, she could propose all she wanted.

"We need to hire a hunter to take care of the feral hogs. Trent won't let Alissa even play in the yard and the ranch hands are getting anxious. And Kelly is out of her mind. The hogs have been chewing on her gazebo and ruining the landscape for her pictures. Janice is worried about opening her women's retreat with them wandering around. And my father is taking it upon himself to flush them out so he can shoot them."

"Okay, okay. I get it. You're up to your ass in hogs." He refrained from telling her "I told you so."

"I'm assistant manager of the ranch and I have full authority from my family to offer to lease you the same property, at the same rate as before. Except there's one small difference."

Donovan crushed the flutter of hope in his chest. She was going to ask for something crazy, like he had to shoot to wound the hogs or something like that. "I'm listening," he said huskily.

"No more hunts."

"You don't have to worry about Otto. I wouldn't work for them ever again."

"Would you work for me?"

He leaned back in his chair as their food came. Donovan watched her as she dug into her VLT sandwich. "I can't risk it. Risk you. Sooner or later, I'm going to piss you off and you're going to put yourself in danger again. Sweetheart, it's just not worth it."

"I'm up to my ass in hogs, Donovan."

He felt his lips twitch and speared a meatless ball and ate it before she charmed him into agreeing to give her everything she wanted. He blinked in surprise. Hot damn, that was a good meatless ball. He took another one and thought about it while he chewed. "What the hell am I going to do with the hunting lodge if there aren't any more hunts?"

"We're going to have safari events. I plan on marketing this to schools and local environmentalist groups. Kelly has been taking some pictures—when she can convince Nate or Trent to ride shotgun. I think we could get bird-watchers and all sorts of clubs."

"You've thought this over. And what happens after I get the hogs under control?"

"That's up to you. I trust you. I should have trusted you more, but I thought I was doing the right thing. My intentions were good, but I guess that's why the road to hell is paved with them." She reached over and grabbed his hand. "I'm going to fuck up again. I'm just not going to do it on the wrong end of rifle. Please give me another chance. Give us a chance."

He was more than willing to do that. And if the safari thing didn't work out, they'd figure something out. "Anything else I should know about?"

"You don't get a three-year lease."

"I need at least a three-year lease to make my money back and still have a profit to live off on when I move on."

"You get a twenty-five-year lease or the deal is off."

He blinked at her. "Do I look like a cell company?"

"You look like someone I don't want to let go. Of course, my father thought of a more cost-effective proposal, if you'd like to hear that."

"I'm all ears, sweetheart."

"You could marry me."

Donovan grinned. "Are you proposing to me?"

"Do I have to get down on one knee?"

He wanted to marry her. To hell with the land. But marrying him came with baggage. "Are you forgetting who might be sauntering up to our property one day?"

"Wouldn't you rather be there when he did?"

"I'd rather he didn't show up at all, but yeah. I want to be with you. For more than twenty-five years. For all the time we have. I've been miserable these past weeks. I thought you hated everything about me, except for the good parts." He kissed her knuckles.

"I could never hate you."

"Even if I may sometimes have to kill animals?"

She sighed. "I don't like it. But I can live with it, because I don't want to live without you."

"Then, yes, Emily Sullivan, I will do the honor of becoming your husband. If you will do the honor of being my bride."

"That's it?" Emily teased. "You're not getting down on

one knee?"

"You're going to have to wait for the ring before I do that."

"Will I have to wait long?"

"You don't strike me as the patient type," he drawled.

"I can be very patient." She touched his knee under the table. "I'm being very patient right now."

"Finish your lunch."

"Why don't we get it to go?"

Chapter Nineteen

CARRIE WAS A good waitress, but she was taking forever boxing their stuff up.

"I'll be in the truck," Emily said, grabbing his keys.

"What are you up to?"

"Come find out." She gave him what she hoped was a sexy smile and sauntered out to his truck. Climbing in, she slid off her panties and her bra as discreetly as she could and slipped them into her purse.

Donovan jogged to the truck and stowed the bags of food behind his seat. "Change your mind about coming back to the hotel?" he asked, shutting the door.

She slid over to him and kissed him before he started the truck. Taking his hand, she guided it up under her skirt. Then she took his other one and pushed it up under her shirt.

Groaning, he rolled her nipple between his finger and thumb. "You're trying to kill me, aren't you?"

"Drive fast or I'll fuck you in this truck," she said against his mouth.

Donovan tugged on her nipple while kissing her thoroughly. His other hand had flipped up her skirt and he trailed his fingertips over the globes of her ass.

"Start the car," she ordered him, as she unbuttoned his pants.

Donovan stopped her with a choked laugh. "Sweetheart, if it wasn't broad daylight, I'd already be fucking you. But buckle up, because I'm going to break the sound barrier getting us to my hotel room."

Emily sat back in her seat, but kept her skirt up.

"Trying to drive me crazy?" he asked, taking advantage of the stoplight to trace his fingers between her legs.

"Is it working?" she breathed, leaning into the sweet caress that was over too soon as the truck lurched forward again.

Pulling into the Bluebonnet Inn parking lot, Donovan lunged across the seat and kissed her before breaking it off and cursing. "Inside. It may be up against the door, but it's going to be inside without an audience."

Emily stumbled out of the truck and ran to keep up with him. She was barely through the door before Donovan slammed it closed and hauled her up against it.

"You want to tease?" He unbuckled his pants, took a condom out of his pocket, and rolled it down over his cock.

She wrapped her legs around his waist and cried out when he plunged inside her. "Yes." Spreading her arms out flat, she stretched against him as he fucked her hard against the door. Each thrust filled her with delicious friction. She was wet and swollen and needed every inch of him.

Pulling up her shirt, he sunk deep in her and held himself there while taking her nipple in his mouth and sucking hard on it.

"Move damn you," she shrieked, lifting her hips up.

Donovan threw his head back and laughed. "So demanding."

"Weeks," she panted. "It's been weeks. Go slow later. I need you now."

He took her hard and fast, covering her mouth with his palm when she got loud. Emily screamed her orgasm into it, and he shook apart shortly after. They leaned, panting against the door, until Emily's legs collapsed and she sank to the ground.

"Now go slow," she said. Her lips felt puffy as she took off his clothes. Emily kissed his broad chest, licking his nipples and then down to his abs.

"Give me a second," he said, lifting her back to his mouth. He took off her shirt and skirt and laid her on the bed. "Be right back." Donovan went into the bathroom to dispose of the condom and clean up a bit.

He was back before she could miss him too much. "Touch me," she begged. "Don't ever stop."

"I couldn't. Not now. Not ever." He lay down on the bed next to her and she eagerly grabbed his thick cock and rubbed it up and down. She loved the velvet feel in her hands and when his fingers touched her intimately, she sighed.

"Just like that."

He had a magic touch and rubbed her slowly. Each time his finger brushed her clit, she gasped and offered him her breasts to taste and lick. Meanwhile, she stroked him with long easy pulls. As the fever and tension built inside her, he tickled her faster and sucked harder on her nipples.

"Fuck me," she demanded.

"Soon," he promised in a growly voice that sent her over the edge.

Panting, she rode his fingers as she came and pushed him on his back. But before she could straddle him, he rolled her underneath him. Teasing her, he slid his cock up and down her drenched pussy.

"I want you inside me again."

He pressed burning kisses on her stomach down to her thighs. At the first touch of his tongue, Emily bolted upright and reached for him. "I want to taste you, too."

Rolling again, Donovan settled her on top of him. Emily scurried around so her breasts were pressed against his stomach. He slid her down on his mouth, clutching her ass.

It felt so good—she let him explore her with his tongue before she went down on him. Emily sucked his cock into her mouth and matched his rhythm of licking. Her fingers clutched his legs and she shook from the tremors he was stirring up with his moans and kisses.

He was deep in her throat when the lightning flickering of his tongue sent her over the edge into a squirming, screaming orgasm. Easing her off him, he slid out of her mouth and put on a condom. She was boneless from ecstasy, barely able to move. Donovan came around from behind and eased her up to her hands and knees.

Pushing into her, he grabbed her hips and pulled her back. Emily groaned and stretched, needing him to move, hoping he would go deep. He did, rolling his hips slowly against her. Donovan moved her hips where he wanted them, back hard against him and then easing away.

He played with her like this. She was boneless and unwilling to stop him. He fucked her steady and with his entire length. Soon, she was quivering in reaction. She felt him in every inch of her and she clamped down on him to keep him there.

"That feels like heaven, sweetheart," he breathed. "You feel amazing."

"Love you," she whispered. "Love you so much."

Donovan groaned and thrust into her hard. "Love you, too. I can't get enough of you." He increased the pace and Emily gripped the bedsheets, unable to do anything but hang on and feel the luscious sensations of his body pleasuring hers.

He came with a roar and held her tight against him, pressing kisses along her spine. Pulling out, he collapsed on his back.

Cuddling up next to him, Emily said, "I can't wait to spend the next twenty-five years or more doing exactly this."

"It's a deal."

"No matter what happens with the ranch, promise me that we'll be together?" Emily lifted her head up to look at him.

"I promise," Donovan said, with a satiated smile on his face.

Epilogue

"TAKE THE PICTURE," Emily said between her teeth.

She was dressed in white and silver cowboy boots with a Mexican cotton dress that was hand-embroidered in shades of red and turquoise. Donovan was dressed in black, with a crisp white shirt and a black onyx bolo tie.

"Move to the left. I want to hide the damage the hogs did to the side of the gazebo," Kelly said, adjusting the camera on the tripod.

Stifling a sigh, Emily shuffled to the left with her arms still around Donovan.

"Donovan, get your hand off her ass," Kelly said.

"I like his hand on my ass."

"Not for the engagement pictures. Come on. I've got to give Aunt Candace something to work with or she'll have my… Holy shit… Don't move."

"If it's a hog, my rifle's in the truck." Donovan took a step forward.

"I said don't move." Kelly used her *Mommy has had enough of your shit* voice. They froze in place. Kelly took the camera off the tripod, working fast.

"Smile, damn it."

Emily pasted on a smile, feeling confused.

Kelly sidestepped and starting clicking pictures as fast as she could. "Open your eyes, damn it, and give me a real smile."

"I feel like we're on a runway or something," Donovan said.

Then Kelly turned the camera completely away from them and moved forward.

Emily turned and nearly fell on her ass. If it hadn't been for Donovan's hand there, she might have. Ghost was casually sauntering by without a care in the world.

"I don't fucking believe it," Donovan muttered.

Emily laughed. They had looked everywhere, but they had been looking in the wrong place. She wasn't deep in Donovan's woods, she was hanging around the cattle pastures by Janice's retreat building. She would be far away from the hunters if she kept to this side of the property.

Ghost headed down the trail behind Janice's retreat building and disappeared into the forest.

"Tell me you got that?" Emily rushed to Kelly's side where she was reviewing the shots.

"That's one hell of a photo bomb." Kelly showed her a picture of them standing by the gazebo with Ghost calmly walking in the background.

"That's good luck, right?" Emily and Kelly hugged each other.

"Janice is going to flip," Kelly said. "I'm going to follow her and see if I can get some more candids."

"Let me grab my rifle in case there's trouble." Donovan

headed to the truck.

"You can't go in like that. You'll destroy your suit."

"I can't take the time to change. We might miss her again." He opened the door and took out his rifle. He loaded it quickly and hurried after Kelly.

"I can't ruin these boots," Emily wailed. "Do you know how hard it is to find good boots that aren't made out of leather?"

Donovan kissed her as he passed by. "Who wears white cowboy boots on a ranch anyway? It's just a matter of time before they get dirty."

"To hell with it," she said, following him. She hoped she didn't fall down in her pretty white dress, but it would be worth it to get another glimpse of the ranch's good luck charm.

The End

If you enjoyed this book, please leave a review at your favorite online retailer! Even if it's just a sentence or two it makes all the difference.

Thanks for reading *The Cowboy's Hunt* by Jamie K. Schmidt!

Discover your next romance at TulePublishing.com.

If you enjoyed *The Cowboy's Hunt*,
you'll love the next book in....

The Three Sisters Ranch series

Book 1: *The Cowboy's Daughter*

Book 2: *The Cowboy's Hunt*

Book 3: *The Cowboy's Heart*
Coming November 2019!

Available now at your favorite online retailer!

If you enjoyed *The Cowboy's Hunt*, you'll love the other books in Tule's Last Stand series!

A Son for the Texas Cowboy
by Sinclair Jayne

Homecoming for the Cowboy
by Nicole Helm

Sweet on the Cowboy
by Sasha Summers

Available now at your favorite online retailer!

About the Author

USA Today bestselling author, Jamie K. Schmidt, writes erotic contemporary love stories and paranormal romances. Her steamy, romantic comedy, Life's a Beach, reached #65 on USA Today, #2 on Barnes & Noble and #9 on Amazon and iBooks. Her Club Inferno series from Random House's Loveswept line has hit both the Amazon and Barnes & Noble top one hundred lists. The first book in the series, Heat, put her on the USA Today bestseller list for the first time, and is a #1 Amazon bestseller. Her book Stud is a 2018 Romance Writers of America Rita® Finalist in Erotica. Her dragon paranormal romance series has been called "fun and quirky" and "endearing." Partnered with New York Times bestselling author and former porn actress, Jenna Jameson, Jamie's hardcover debut, SPICE, continues Jenna's FATE trilogy.

Visit her website at jamiekschmidt.weebly.com

Thank you for reading

The Cowboy's Hunt

If you enjoyed this book, you can find more from all our great authors at TulePublishing.com, or from your favorite online retailer.

Made in the USA
Columbia, SC
12 May 2020

96809430R00131